# THE GREEN ROOM

Janet Sierzant

La Maison Publishing, Inc.
Vero Beach, Florida
The Hibiscus City
www.lamaisonpublishing.com

Maison

*Beware of the greatest love, for it has the highest potential to hurt you.*

# Chapter 1 | The Stranger

The rumbling of an engine woke Dona Pearson from a deep sleep. At first, she thought it was the train. It was only two blocks away from her building. When she moved into her apartment, she hadn't realized how close it was. It was so loud that she considered moving, but soon adjusted to the sound.

It took a moment to realize the noise wasn't coming from the tracks. It was coming from the street. The sound of a motorcycle reverberated in her ears. Dona wasn't a fan of two-wheeled vehicles—the loud rubble made her brain feel chaotic. The sound grew louder and then stopped. Compelled to check it out, she rushed to the window and pulled the blind aside to peek through the slats. It was dark, except for the yellow circles of light emanating from the streetlights. A man stood by the curb wearing a black leather jacket, even though it was much too hot for Florida. He scribbled something on a small pad, tucked it into his pocket, and rode away into the night—the roar of his motorcycle became a whisper in the heavy summer air. She went to the front room, which overlooked the parking lot, and scanned the shadows of the night. Nothing—she tried to go back to sleep.

*****

The alarm clock beeped, and Dona hit the snooze button, then hit it twice before realizing that if she did it again, she'd be late for work.

Caught in rush hour, Dona navigated through traffic, swerving in and out of the lanes. Glancing in the side view mirror, she noticed a black Impala following too closely. It was hard to see the driver through the dark glass.

"Slow down!" she shouted, but he continued to follow her. She cut in front of the car to her right and sped through a red light. Horns blared as she struggled to keep control of her vehicle.

By the time Dona reached the office, the car had already left. She pulled into the underground parking garage and whipped into her usual spot under the light. The car's automatic locks echoed through the garage when she pressed the remote button. As Dona walked toward the elevator, she heard footsteps rushing behind her. Her heart pounded like it might jump out of her chest until she realized it was Ted, the HR manager. Catching up with her, he pushed the button for the elevator.

"Good morning, beautiful. You look nice today." Ted's eyes were fixed on her breasts.

Realizing her blouse revealed too much cleavage, Dona pulled her jacket closed.

The elevator doors opened, and they stepped inside. Dona's office was on the fourth floor. Luckily,

Ted worked on the second. Before exiting, he turned, preventing the doors from closing again with his foot.

"Would you like to have lunch with me?"

"I'm sorry, Ted. I don't think I'll be taking lunch today. I have too much work."

"You're always busy," Ted said with a hint of annoyance.

After the doors closed, she breathed a sigh of relief, recalling the first time they had met at the Community Health Center. She didn't know anyone yet. Ted had slate-gray eyes and a flirty smile. Every day, he came to her department and asked unabashed questions about her life, getting a kick from her reactions. He'd laugh and say, "Just kidding." Most of the other employees didn't like his brand of humor, but she had grown accustomed to his jovial manner. When he asked her out to lunch, she didn't have the heart to say no. He seemed harmless.

After that, he assumed they were a couple, but Dona wasn't interested. She tried to let him down gently, but that only made him think he could change her mind. Ted was persistent. He was sweet in his pursuit, but it turned sour when he didn't get what they wanted. It was always the same with men. It wasn't that she was particularly beautiful. Her mousy brown hair, thin lips, and curved nose didn't feel attractive at all. Maybe it was something in her eyes. They zeroed in on her insecurities. Men wanted to be heroes — to rescue the damsel in distress. She came across as timid and abiding, but Dona was quite capable of caring for herself.

# Chapter 2 | Abduction

At five o'clock, Dona looked at a stack of personal information for six new patients. She debated whether to work late or go home. With no reason to rush home, she decided to stay and finish her work.

Helen waved as she left the office. "Staying late again, Dona?"

"You know me. I don't like leaving things unfinished."

Her coworker laughed. "I'll see you in the morning."

Everyone had gone. The office was quiet. Feeling lonely, Dona picked up her cell phone to call David, but hung up before the first ring could be heard. He had been pressuring her for months to move in with him, but their relationship wasn't going anywhere— they just weren't compatible.

Then, staring at the phone, she noticed an incoming text message. "When are we going out on another date?"

It was from Ted. He had become a nuisance. Dona had warned him to leave her alone, or she'd report him to upper management. If she reported him, it would be the second time he was written up for sexual harassment. He begged her not to tell anyone, or he'd lose his job. Against her better judgment, Dona said she wouldn't if he promised to leave her alone. He did for a while, but gradually resumed pestering her.

Rubbing her eyes, she looked up at the clock. It was almost nine. She shoved the two unfinished files back into their folders, reached for her purse, and headed for the elevator. When she pressed the button, the elevator doors opened immediately. She looked down the hall, but there was no one there.

The parking garage looked different at night—foreboding. Keys ready, she walked briskly to her car, the clip-clop of her heels echoing as she walked. Sensing she wasn't alone, she quickened her pace and then stopped. The only sound was the hum of a fluorescent light flickering overhead, as if it were deciding whether to stay lit or burn out.

"Mike? Is that you?"

No one answered. *Where the hell is that security guard when I need him?*

Just as Dona lifted her hand to open the car door, she noticed her front tire was flat. The hair on the back of her neck stood up. *Quick! Get in the car!* Her brain screamed. But it was too late. An arm wrapped around her chest, and a man's hand covered her mouth with a foul-smelling cloth. Her legs buckled. Her eyes blurred, and the lights dimmed.

*****

Dona jolted awake with shooting pain in her head.

*Where am I?* It was dark. The grumble of an engine filled her ears. She tried to focus in the darkness, realizing she was trapped in the trunk of a car. She tried to move, but her hands and legs were bound. She tugged at the ties and winced.

"Help," Dona tried to yell through a piece of tape that covered her mouth. She let out a muffled scream, thrashing against the restraints. Her body bounced and jolted with every bump, stop, and sharp turn. She gasped as pain radiated from her spine to her shoulders.

The vehicle slowed, and the engine turned off. There was a clicking sound, and the smell of gas fumes entered the trunk, making it harder to breathe. An unrelenting pressure was suddenly squeezing the air out of her lungs. Adrenaline surged through her drug-induced fog. Lifting her legs, she kicked on the lid of the trunk with her feet in a frantic attempt to draw someone's attention. The fueling stopped. Then the engine roared back to life, and the car sped off. Her heart sank. She slowed her breathing with deliberate short spurts and tried to remain calm. She remembered hearing about a woman shoved into a trunk by a man in the supermarket parking lot. She had pulled up the carpet looking for the wires connected to the trunk release and escaped. The woman wrote to the major automotive companies, attempting to persuade them to install emergency latches in the trunks of their new cars. Ford was the first to install the release in its vehicles, but it wasn't long before other automakers followed suit. Locating the illuminated T-shaped handle, she wiggled her body against the side to reach it. *Next time the car stops, I'll be ready. Please – let someone see me.*

The vehicle continued for hours, and the air grew chilly. Dona sensed that she was no longer in the South. The cold made her teeth chatter uncontrollably. She thought they might shatter at any moment. Lack of circulation made her fingertips tingle – needles and pins were poking her skin. Sweat rolled down the side of her face – or was it tears?

The car slowed again and came to a stop. Footsteps on the gravel grew louder as someone approached the back of the vehicle. With her fingers on the lever, she jerked herself up and pulled. The lid popped open. A rush of fresh air entered the trunk, and she hungrily breathed in. The foul-smelling cloth covered her nose. She fought to keep conscious, but it was useless.

She felt herself floating through the air as her mind faded away.

# Chapter 3 | Dark and Dank

Dona woke with a start, thinking she was in David's bed. Instead, she was lying on a concrete floor. Dampness surrounded her like a heavy blanket, and a chill ran down her spine. She opened her eyes and tried to lift her head from the clammy pillow, but a throbbing headache pinned her down. A wool blanket was under her. Although the blindfold and tape were gone, the smell of dirt, stagnant water, and musty air made it hard to breath. The taste of bile filled her mouth. She pushed it down. Resisting the urge to vomit, she focused on the single lightbulb suspended from the ceiling until the feeling passed.

Zip ties still dug painfully into her ankles and wrists. She struggled to free herself, but the plastic bit into her skin. Adjusting to the semi-darkness, she rocked herself into a sitting position. She was in a basement.

Across the room, there was a door and, in the corner, a toilet. Dona was about to crawl toward it when she heard footsteps on the stairs. Someone was coming. It made her heart pump harder—so hard it hurt. The only thing she could think to do was play possum. Listening, she waited for the door to open.

Instead, there was a loud scraping sound. Something metal slid across the floor. She squinted at a tray near the door, upon which a bottle of water lay. Her mouth was dry. She needed to quench her thirst, but stayed still in case her captor was still nearby.

The floor above her creaked again, and she thought it safe to move. Creeping toward the tray, the smell of peanut butter made her stomach lurch. Consumed with thirst, she reached for the water bottle with both hands, held it between her knees, and opened the cap with her teeth. It opened easily. Instinctively, she pushed it away until thirst won. She gulped the warm liquid, spilling half down her chin.

A roach scurried across the floor. Where there was one, there were hundreds. Dona cringed and pushed the tray farther away with the heel of her foot. Roaches scattered in different directions, and two boldly crept toward her. There was no escaping them. *One might even crawl into my mouth while I was sleeping!* With that thought in mind, she tried to breathe through her nose. Curled in a fetal position, she wrapped her arms around her legs for warmth, straining to catch the faintest sound of his return.

She looked around the concrete prison for something sharp. Noticing a jagged crack in the foundation that widened by the building's weight, she scooted to it and slowly rubbed the plastic tie against it. Excruciating pain radiated up her arms, and the concrete scraped her skin. Blood dripped down her arm, and the lime dust burned into her open lesions. Drained, she slumped back against the wall.

As the burning in her wrists subsided, she examined the crack in the concrete again. This time, more determined to free her hands, she sobbed, ignoring the pain, and rubbed her hands up and down on the sharp edge. Each drop of blood increased her determination to free herself. The tie around her wrist snapped, rewarding her efforts. Turning her attention to the zip tie around her ankles, she lifted her legs and rubbed the plastic against the jagged wall. The binding broke away, along with some skin on her ankles. She tried to stand but collapsed back to the ground as dizziness made the room spin. Once her head cleared, she tried again. Willing her legs to move, she felt her way along the concrete wall toward the only exit. As she suspected, the door was locked.

Above her, the floorboards creaked under someone's weight. The beat of her heartbeat amplified at the thump of footsteps. *Someone is coming down the stairs!*

A piercing screech came from the other side of the door. *A power saw?*

A few moments later, hammering replaced the buzzing, making her headache worse.

An awful thought entered her mind. *Maybe he's building my coffin!*

The noise stopped, and he went back upstairs. A slot was at the bottom of the door. It resembled a mail slot, but was longer and wider. She pushed open the metal flap to see what was on the other side.

A workbench—not much else was visible under the dim light shining through a small window. Dona heard footsteps again and pulled her hand back too fast. The slot closed with a clang. She hurried back under the blanket, hoping he wouldn't notice she had freed herself.

She sucked in the air and held her breath. Her captor was not far away. Anticipating her demise, she pressed her eyes closed and tried to lie still, wishing the ground would open and swallow her. There was no place to hide. An urge to urinate came over her. She squeezed her legs together and fought it.

The footsteps retreated. Dona opened her eyes and stared at the toilet in the corner of the room. The filthy toilet lacked a seat. Slowly, she tried to get to her feet, finding her legs too shaky. She inched across the concrete. Disgusted, she hiked up her skirt and pulled down her panties. She raised herself by grasping the edge of the bowl. Her legs were weak as she tried to straddle the bowl. Unsure how long she could hover like that, she focused on peeing, but her legs gave out, and she fell to the floor. Lying in her urine, she pulled her panties up and crawled back to the wall. A chill seeped into her bones, and she trembled.

She turned her attention to the tray and summoned the courage to crawl to it. A few roaches were feeding on the peanut butter sandwich. Surrendering to her hunger, she shooed the bugs away and picked up the sandwich delicately, debating whether to eat it. She hurried back to the cold concrete wall. After making sure there were no hitchhikers on the sandwich, she gritted her teeth and bit into the stale bread. The peanut butter stuck to the roof of her mouth. She couldn't swallow. Nibbling the edge of the bread, she let it dissolve in her mouth. Washing it down with some water, she used the rest to rinse the blood off her wrists and ankles.

A sickening feeling rose in her throat, and she broke into a cold sweat. The walls of the basement swirled around her. Convinced that she was about to vomit, she tried to crawl to the toilet. Her knees scraped on the freezing concrete as she struggled across the rough floor. She stopped where she was and spewed vomit across the floor. Her throat burned as if in flames. She tried to push herself up but fell flat on her face. Too dizzy to move any further, she put her head on her arms and breathed through the pain coursing throughout her head. The needy little child inside her whined, *Why didn't I stay with David?*

The basement walls melted away, but she fought to stay awake. Trapped between sleeping and dreaming, she felt her body rise from the dark, dank place where she lay.

# Chapter 4 | The Green Room

Dona opened her swollen, gritty eyes and adjusted to the light as shapes began to take form. The scent of fresh paint overwhelmed her.

"Where am I?"

She wasn't in the basement anymore. Disoriented, she tried to get her bearings. Slowly, she sat up in the king-sized bed and looked around. The room looked comfortable, giving the illusion that she was in a safe place. The walls were a putrid green shade, the trim white, though parts of it were missing. She noticed two doors across the room. One had the same mail slot at the bottom as the door in the basement. She rubbed her wrists, relieved that he hadn't bound her again.

An old-fashioned alarm clock ticking softly on a nightstand. Across the room were a dresser and a table with a computer on it. Dark green curtains framed the mini blinds. Dona pushed off the green and white floral comforter and slid out of bed. A bolt of pain shot through her foot and brought her to her knees. Clutching the side of the bed, she pulled herself up and staggered to the window. When she yanked on the cord, the curtains parted, and she found herself staring at a green wall. There was no window. She turned to the computer and pressed the power button. *Perhaps I can find help online.* She double-clicked on the browser. A message popped up: 'No internet connection detected.' Her heart sank.

Legs shaking, she limped to the first door and turned the knob. The door was locked. She tried pushing the slot outward to see what was on the other side. It didn't budge. The second door led to a bathroom with a toilet, sink, and shower stall—no window. She stared at her reflection in the small mirror above the sink. Her shoulder-length hair was matted with blood, making her blonde highlights appear more like her naturally brown hair, which matched her eyes.

"Good morning, Dona." A muffled voice startled her. It sounded electronically altered, as if the man were underwater.

She looked around the room and spotted a small black box hanging in the corner alongside a surveillance camera.

"How do you know my name?"

He laughed.

She realized then—she wasn't just some random woman.

"What do you want from me?"

"I want you to make yourself comfortable. You're going to be here for a long time."

"Who the hell are you?"

"I'm someone you dismissed—a piece of trash. All I ever wanted was for you to love me, but you wouldn't give me a chance. You never had time for me in your life. Well, now things have changed. You have all the time in the world."

"Let me out!"

"All in good time. All in good time," he said, followed by a devilish laugh.

"Who are you?" She screamed.

"Turn on the computer," he instructed.

She limped to the desk and pressed the power button again. The screen lit up, and a man appeared sitting at a desk wearing a ski mask.

"That's better," he said. "Now, we can talk face-to-face. I apologize for going to such lengths, but it was the only way I could get your attention."

"Let me go," she pleaded.

"I'm afraid I can't do that."

"What are you going to do to me?"

"Don't worry, my love. I won't hurt you."

"You already have." Dona examined the abrasions on her wrists and ankles. The wound on her ankle throbbed, red with infection.

"There are first aid supplies in the bathroom," he said, feigning compassion, and jerked his chin toward the bathroom.

"You'll also find clean clothes in the dresser." The screen turned black.

Dona limped to the bathroom and opened the medicine cabinet, fully stocked with supplies: peroxide, Band-Aids, gauze, and a tube of Neosporin.

She did her best to dress the wounds, then struggled back to the bed and cried into one of the fluffy white pillows. "I want to go home," she begged, but there was no answer.

Home? Where was that?

The slot in the door opened, and a tray slid in.

*Food!* Although her stomach was empty, the pain far surpassed her hunger. Still, she was very thirsty. With unsteady legs, she crossed the room to the tray. There was a hamburger, greasy fries, and a milkshake from McDonald's—no water.

Her mouth felt parched. She drank the shake quickly, then crawled between the sheets, racking her brain, trying to recall who she might have angered so horribly in her life. Who would do this to her? *Could it be someone I know?* She couldn't pinpoint someone who might hate her, but a few possible suspects had come to mind. Any of them could have wished her harm.

She recalled a few days earlier, when a woman approached her outside the building as she arrived home from work.

"Are you Dona?"

"Yes, how do you know my name?"

"Someone was asking about you yesterday."

"Me? Are you sure?"

"He asked me if I knew you. I told him no."

"What did this guy look like?"

"He was of average height and on the skinny side. Oh, and he had dark hair. I couldn't see his eyes. He was wearing sunglasses."

"Did he say what he wanted?"

"No, but he gave me the creeps. It's a good thing you need a key to get into our buildings."

"I can't think of any reason someone would be asking about me, but if you see him again, please let me know."

"I will. By the way, I'm Candace. I live in building D."

"Hi, Candace. Glad to meet you."

Dona entered her apartment and double-bolted the door.

Ted's face flashed through her mind. Creepy Ted. *Could it be him?* He always complained that she didn't have time for him. He had access to the personnel records and obtained her work address. She occasionally spotted his car at the corner where she lived. He seemed to show up wherever she went — the grocery store, the library, and even the movies. She sensed it wasn't a coincidence. Eventually, he moved on and set his sights on another woman in the accounts payable department. Afterward, he remained cordial, but she sensed resentment behind his cold, steely gray eyes. Dona brushed it off and gave him the benefit of the doubt. She failed to see the evil that lurked within some people.

# Chapter 5 | Born to Be Wild

## The Green Room

---

"Good morning!"

Dona sat up in bed. When the man appeared on the screen, she moved closer to the computer, searching for clues. Although his image was grainy, there was something familiar about *him*. She gazed at the eyes behind the mask, cold and lifeless, like those of a shark. The furnishings behind him were a mixture of sixties and seventies orange velour and heavy, drab brown curtains. Next to a small table, a cane with an eagle-head grip leaned against the wall.

"Tell me," he said. "What makes you tick?"

"I don't know what you mean."

"I mean, what is it that makes you happy? What do you want?"

"I want to be free," she snapped.

"What do you want from a relationship?"

"That's a stupid question. What does anyone want from a relationship—love, mutual respect, compatibility."

"What type of man is compatible?"

"Someone completely different from *you*!" The

words slipped out of her mouth before she could catch herself.

"That's obvious — and also the reason you're here," he snapped.

"I could have left you in the basement," he barked.

Losing his composure, he paced back and forth across the room, mumbling to himself as he paced out of the camera's range. He was visibly beginning to unspool.

She regretted her outburst, realizing how foolish it was to provoke the man who held all the power. She wanted to scream, but what good would it do?

His pacing slowed, his breathing evened out.

"But you can't blame me for being upset."

"No, I guess not." The screen turned black.

*"Born to Be Wild"* filtered through the walls.

"Let me out, you psycho!" Dona screamed.

The music increased in volume. Realizing she had poked the bear, Dona tried to use psychology.

"I'm sorry I called you that," she said, directing her voice toward the speaker. The volume decreased.

Dona hobbled to the bathroom, where she found an assortment of toiletries. On the sink lay a tube of toothpaste and a new toothbrush. She ripped open the package and brushed her teeth for a long time, trying to scrub away the gritty film.

He'd provided a new bar of soap, shampoo, and conditioner in the shower — everything she needed. She looked around to see if he had planted another camera. Seeing none, she turned on the shower faucet and began undressing. Standing under the warm stream of water, she watched swirls of blood and filth circle the drain. The cuts on her ankles stung as the water hit the wound, but it also felt good.

When she stepped out of the shower, she realized she hadn't taken clean clothes from the dresser.

*Damn!* She wasn't about to walk out there naked, so she pulled her dirty clothes back on and returned to the bedroom. The top drawer was filled with lingerie, the second with shirts, and the third with pants. The clothes were exactly her size. He'd thought of everything. Apparently, this was going to be her home until he decided otherwise. She returned to the bathroom to pull on a pair of jeans and a T-shirt. When she came out, she saw another food tray by the door — peanut butter and jelly. Again. She had always loved PBJs when she was a kid, but now, they made her stomach turn.

The question swirled around in her brain. *What do I want in a relationship?* Although her parents didn't have a great relationship, she still held out the hope that her soulmate was somewhere out there. She wanted to be a wife and a mother. It seemed like a safe goal — with the right man.

# Chapter 6 | Green-Eyed Monster

### *Angelo*

---

Dona began to reflect on her past relationships, starting with Angelo. He was one of the cute boys who hung out at the deli. He never noticed her, so she was surprised when she ran into him at the mall and he asked her out. The dating moved swiftly. They were an attractive couple. Angelo, with his dark curly hair, and Dona, with her Mediterranean complexion. He became her first boyfriend and a permanent fixture in her life. She felt terrible for him when she heard about his childhood. He and his younger brother had suffered abuse at his father's hands. After enduring many black eyes and broken bones, his father threw him down a flight of stairs, landing him in the hospital. His mother filed for a divorce.

"Let's go to my room," he said one evening.

Dona glanced over at his mother, engrossed in a television show. She didn't seem interested in her son's activities.

She followed him upstairs, then Angelo locked the door and kissed her on the lips so suddenly that her head spun. His breath was sweet, and his tongue searched for hers. When his hands wandered up the back of her shirt, she whispered, "Stop."

"What's wrong? Have you been seeing someone else?"

"Don't be silly. It's just that—well—I want to wait until I'm married."

"Then we'll get married!"

"Really?"

"Yes, consider us engaged."

His kisses heated to a fever pitch as he peeled her clothes away and guided her onto his bed. Dona didn't want to lose her virginity, but she felt obligated since she had agreed to come to his room.

"Don't worry, my love. I won't hurt you."

Dona closed her eyes. All she knew about sex was what she had seen in the movies—expecting an earthquake or, at the very least, a tremor. Instead, she felt a stabbing pain—then it was over, ending her virginity at the tender age of seventeen.

Angelo suggested that they rent an apartment together. She liked the idea of going out on her own, but her mother tried to discourage her.

"I have a bad feeling about that boy," she said. "He's too possessive. Don't think that I haven't noticed how he treats you. I don't like him."

"I'm almost eighteen years old, Mom. I think it's time I get on my own."

"He's a jealous man," she warned. "Men like that don't change. They get worse."

"Don't worry. It will be fine. Angelo loves me."

With a false sense of independence, she moved in

with him. In reality, all she did was change her living arrangements. Instead of living under her parents' roof, she was now under Angelo's rules.

Angelo was a control freak with a tendency to fly into jealous rages. The pettiest things would spark a fight. It wasn't long before his true character emerged.

He seemed to change whenever he had too much to drink, and a different side of him revealed itself. Dona ignored each red flag that waved right in front of her eyes and heart. He accused her of flirting with a young man who lived upstairs from them. No matter how much she denied it, he persisted.

Dona started to dread the holidays. Angelo had a way of turning a happy event into a tearful tragedy. For her birthday, he took her to an Italian restaurant. The parking attendant recognized her from high school and gave her a hug.

"I guess he must find you irresistible," Angelo kidded. But she detected a touch of jealousy behind his words.

"What? What did you say?" Dona asked. His accusations disturbed her.

"I see the way guys look at you."

"Just because a man looks at me doesn't mean I'm looking back."

"Never mind."

Her explanation appeased him, but his aggression simmered beneath the surface. Usually, his jealousy only appeared when he was drunk. If she threatened to walk out, he'd break down and apologize, blaming it on the alcohol.

At the beach, he noticed guys staring at her and ordered her to drape a blanket around her bikini-clad body. She felt trapped by his ridiculous jealousy.

Her mother sensed something was wrong, even though Dona tried to hide it. She was like a duck peeking into boiling water — realizing the danger too late.

Angelo watched her every move and restricted visits from her family and friends, complaining that she spent too much time with them and not enough with him. He always wanted her under his reign. She drank coffee and chain-smoked at the kitchen table, playing solitaire until the cards were faded and curled on the edges. He was abusive, especially when he had a few drinks. Sometimes it was just a slap or a push, but it wore her down each time. She sank into a deep depression. Her appetite disappeared, and she began to lose weight.

"What you need is a baby," Angelo said.

*What I need are birth control pills.*

\*\*\*\*\*

Dona took the pills, and her stomach stayed flat, and Angelo began to get suspicious.

Even though she hid the pills in a sock at the back of her dresser drawer, she constantly worried he'd find them.

Every day was the same. Angelo drank beer and sat in front of the television. One night, as he slammed down a six-pack, he said, "Let's make a baby."

"Please. I'm not in the mood."

Ignoring her pleas, he pulled her toward the bedroom. She gave in, letting him have his way, but it felt like she'd been raped. She knew that was ridiculous. *How could it be rape if I let him?*

A month later, Dona missed her period. Panicked, she counted the pills in her case, thinking she might have forgotten to take some. The count was correct. Angelo came up behind her. "Don't worry. They're *only* sugar pills." He tilted his head, his black eyes as soulless as pieces of coal. "Did you think you could fool me?"

"No, I just..."

"I just!" He mimicked. "I just didn't want your baby. Isn't that what you were thinking?"

"No. Of course, I want your baby."

"Liar!"

Dona had seen his temper before, but this was different. He slapped the side of her head — the blow sent her to her knees. She clutched the doorframe to rise to her feet. Trembling, she rushed to the kitchen and grabbed the receiver to call her father. "Dad" — was all she could say before Angelo pulled the phone cord out of the wall. He grabbed her by the throat and hit her with the receiver. Blood trickled down the side of her face. Angelo came at her again. She tried to kick him in the groin but missed, getting him on the knee.

Bleeding and disoriented, she ran back to the bedroom.

"You bitch. You dislocated my knee."

Hobbling after her, Angelo grasped the nape of her

neck and threw her onto the bed.

"No, don't," she begged as he tore off her panties. She was no match for his strength.

When it was over, Angelo passed out on the bed, so she slipped away to the bathroom, finding her eye swollen. Dried blood pooled at the corner of her lip.

There was a loud knock on the door. "Dona? It's Dad. Let me in."

Angelo's eyes sprang open, and he jumped up, but she beat him to the door.

"What the hell's going on here?" her father demanded after seeing her face.

"This is between us," Angelo sneered.

"Get your things, Dona. You're leaving. And take off that ring."

Angelo's fists were tight at his side. "Dona! Don't you dare leave!"

She twisted the ring once, twice, then set it on the table next to the front door. She grabbed her shoes and didn't stop to put them on.

Just as her father had predicted, Angelo showed up outside their small colonial house a few days later. Dona was alone.

"Dona!" he called.

She crouched under the window with her back against the wall.

"I saw the curtain move. I know you're up there, Dona. Get outside. Now!"

There was a pause.

"I'm sorry. Please! Give me another chance." He appeared to be crying. "I just want to talk to you."

A twinge of pity came over her. For a moment, she wondered if she should go outside to talk. When she peeked out the window, their eyes met.

He shook his fist. "Come out here, or I'm coming in."

Terrified, she ducked down and crawled around the house, locking the doors and windows.

Angelo pounded on the door.

"I'm not going anywhere," he screamed. "You can't avoid me forever."

She thought it would come off its hinges. She ran to the kitchen phone to call the police, then crawled into the closet and waited for the sirens to arrive.

As they took him away, she heard him yell, "If I can't have you, nobody will. You can be sure of that!"

Dona filed harassment charges. The judge granted her a restraining order but released Angelo on bail.

She didn't feel safe and continually looked over her shoulder. She lived in fear until the trial date. Angelo never showed up. Although the police didn't actively look for him, a warrant for his arrest was out. Dona had hoped she was finally off his radar.

# Chapter 7 | Father's Rights

## The Green Room

---

The masked image appeared on the screen. "I see your ankles are healing, but you didn't touch your dinner last night."

"I'm not hungry."

"You need to keep up your strength."

"I don't want your food."

"Suit yourself."

"Who are you?" she bit her lower lip, fighting the urge to curse him.

He ignored her.

"At least tell me your name."

"Call me Joe."

"Please let me go! I won't tell anyone."

He laughed. "Sure, you won't."

"How long do you plan to keep me?"

"As long as it takes." He took a sip of his drink through the ski mask and folded his arms across his chest.

She hated spending another day or night in his room and felt her psychology training slip.

"I don't want to be here. You're a crazy psycho."

She saw his eyes widen, even behind the mask. Joe pounded his fists on the table, spilling his drink.

Jumping to his feet, he knocked the chair over.

"Just answer my questions, damn it!"

Dona had hit a nerve. Cowering, she moved away from the screen.

He waited for her to respond, then sighed.

"It's true. I am holding you here against your will. You might as well get used to it. You have to admit, I've tried my best to make it comfy here, haven't I?"

The word *comfy* felt like a violation. Dona was anything but...

There was no way out unless she told him what he wanted to know.

"So, what is it you want to ask me?"

Joe calmly picked up the chair as if nothing had happened. "I'm sorry if I scared you." He adjusted himself in the chair and sat up straighter. "Well, I thought we could talk about *father's rights*."

Dona smirked. "What is that supposed to mean?"

"I just want to know your opinion. You seem like a woman who doesn't need a man around. What about the children? Don't they deserve to know their father?"

"Not if the father is abusive or never around."

"Even murderers have a right to be called Daddy."

"That's not true. Have you ever killed anyone?"

"Only when provoked."

A chill ran down Dona's spine. She chose her words carefully. "Just because a man deposits his sperm doesn't mean he deserves to be called a father."

"If women didn't use their babies like pawns in a

chess game, they would be more active in their children's lives. Take abortion, for example. It doesn't matter what the father wants. Women make all the rules. They have babies or not, as they please. Why should women decide if a child is born or dies?"

"Just because a woman chose to have an abortion doesn't mean it was her desire. The decision is never easy. The burden is on women. If they go ahead and have a baby with an abusive partner, there could be dire consequences. Besides, not all men are happy to be fathers. Most of them don't even pay child support."

"You women are all alike—always whining. You don't want the father around, but you want the money."

The screen went black. The silence that followed was worse than his voice. Dona stared at her reflection, stunned by how easy he'd peeled back a scar she thought had healed. But it hadn't. The guilt still lived inside her.

She remembered the drive to the Pregnancy Resource Clinic.

# Chapter 8 | Human Nature

## *Angelo*

The Supreme Court decision of Roe v. Wade granted women the right to end their pregnancies. Knowing her parents would be distraught. Dona didn't tell them she was pregnant. She drove to the clinic alone. One block away, traffic was heavy. As she waited at a red light, she noticed the car in front of her had a sign in the rear window: "Baby on board!" She envisioned what the child inside her might look like. Perhaps it would have Angelo's brown eyes or wavy black hair. Reality crashed down on her as the light turned green. Angelo was physically and emotionally abusive. *If he knew I was pregnant, I'd never be free from him.*

She approached the clinic and signaled to turn into the parking lot. A security guard escorted her to the front door.

Apprehensive, she approached the glass partition. It slid open.

"Can I help you?" The receptionist asked.

"I'm here to see about getting an abortion," Dona whispered.

"Fill out this paperwork," she said, handing her a

clipboard.

In case of an emergency, she wrote 911. Dona scribbled her name as sloppily as possible, as if not recognizing her signature would somehow distance her from what she was planning to do.

After returning the forms, she found a chair in the waiting room. The smell of potpourri filled the air. At first, it was soothing, but after a few minutes, she began to feel unwell from the overpowering scent.

Other women sat nearby. No one made eye contact. She flipped through the pages of the Christmas edition of Family Circle. Most of the women featured were dressed in holiday sweaters featuring snowmen and Santas. They smiled up at her accusingly, so she tossed the magazine aside.

Finally, the door opened. "Dona?"

She jumped up and followed a young girl into an office where a middle-aged woman sat behind a desk.

"Hi, I'm Kathy, from St. Andrews Church."

"Church?" Immediately, guilt washed over Dona.

"I'm a volunteer counselor," she said. "The state requires counseling before any procedures. I'm here to help you with your decision. Have a seat, dear."

Dona sat down and nervously rolled the ends of the brochure she had picked up out front.

Kathy looked over her chart.

"Can you tell me the day of your last period?"

"Um." Dona bit her bottom lip hard, hard enough to taste blood.

"That's okay. We'll be able to narrow it down when we do the ultrasound."

"Ultrasound?"

"It's just an image." Rising from her chair, she directed Dona to an examining room and handed her a paper gown. "Someone will be in shortly."

Alone in the room, Dona undressed and climbed onto the table. The door opened, and a technician wheeled a machine into the room. "Hi, I'm Stephanie. I'll be doing your sonogram."

Dona forced a smile.

"Don't be nervous," Stephanie said. "I'm just going to put some jelly on your stomach. It'll be a little cold at first, but it doesn't hurt."

She turned on the monitor, and a steady thump-thump sound filled the room. "That's the baby's heartbeat. Would you like to see the screen?"

"No!" she yelled. "I mean... no, thank you."

"I understand," Stephanie said. She packed up the sonogram equipment. "You can get dressed and go back to Kathy's office."

"Thank you," Dona said, reaching for her clothes.

Kathy was already studying the sonogram results when Dona entered. She smiled. "You're about seven weeks along."

"I can't have this baby!" As the words escaped her lips, Dona felt something inside her soul whimper. It all seemed so unfair.

Ordinarily, she would never consider having an abortion. She wanted to be a mother more than anything, but not with Angelo. He was too abusive. An innocent baby shouldn't have the burden of a violent parent.

"Have you discussed it with the father?"

"No! The father doesn't know."

Kathy tucked her short brown hair behind her ears and stood. "Oh, I see," she whispered. "They'll schedule the procedure out front if you intend to go through with it, but remember, you can always change your mind. God bless you, Dona."

Dona returned to the front desk to schedule the procedure.

"Payment is due on the day of the abortion," the receptionist said. "You'll be having local anesthetic."

"Is it painful?" she asked.

"No, but it's a little uncomfortable. You'll be awake and aware of everything that's going on. The whole thing will take about an hour, but you may have to stay in recovery until you can leave. Don't worry. Unless there are complications, you should be out of here in no time."

*Complications?*

Feeling sick, Dona made the appointment and stuck the paperwork in her purse.

The winter sun was already down, shadows stretching across the dimly lit parking lot. She noticed a man lurking near the side of the building and quickened her pace. Before she made it to her car, he lunged at her and shoved her to the ground.

"Do you think it's going to be that easy to get rid of my child?"

"Angelo?"

"That's my baby you're carrying. I'm not letting you get an abortion. Fathers have rights, you know."

"You're not fit to be a father," she yelled, managing to get back on her feet. "Leave me alone, or I'll call the police."

"Yeah, and by the time they get here, you'll be dead."

She realized her life was in grave danger.

Angelo dragged her by the hair across the parking lot to his car.

Out of the corner of her eye, she spotted two women from the clinic walking toward them.

"Please! Help me!" She broke free and ran toward them.

The two women turned and ran back inside the building. Angelo caught Dona by the hair and shoved her into the car. He put a gun to her head and forced her into the passenger seat over the console. His finger hovered over the trigger as he pointed the barrel at her face. He started the engine and took off down the road.

Lightning flashed, illuminating the clinic as it receded into the distance. Dona glanced in the side mirror. *Oh, God! I hope those women call the police.*

Just then, the sky opened, and rain pounded the windshield like tiny stones.

"Angelo, please. I wasn't going to get an abortion."

"Then what were you doing there?"

"I just came for information."

"You're not being honest with me. Don't you know there's liberation in telling the truth?"

"Please. Don't hurt me—don't hurt our baby. Angelo. I love you." She tried to appease him.

"You do?"

"Yes, please. Let's talk."

A few blocks away, police sirens wailed behind them.

Angelo sped up, his foot pressing hard on the gas. "We're all going to die tonight."

"Please," she begged. "If you stop, I'll tell them you didn't do anything."

A police cruiser raced up behind them, its lights flashing. Angelo drove faster, swerving onto the opposite lane of traffic. Dona could see headlights up ahead and squeezed her eyes shut. *This is the end!*

Up ahead, he spotted a roadblock. Angelo slammed on the brakes, causing the tires to skid and lose their grip. The vehicle hydroplaned on the rain-slicked road as he tried to steer around a tree, but the car spun out of control. Grazing a clump of hedges, it screeched to a stop in a shallow ditch. Another police car pulled in front and blocked them from taking off again.

While Angelo tried to hide the gun under the seat, Dona jumped out of the car. Relieved, she watched as the officers pulled him out, kicking and screaming. Before they handcuffed him, he stabbed his finger at Dona and yelled, "I'll never forgive you."

They loaded him into one of the police cars and took off.

The police insisted on taking her to the E.R., but she refused.

"At least let us escort you home."

"What about my car?"

"We suggest you go back for it in the morning,"

one of the officers said. "You're in no shape to drive tonight."

Shaken and bruised, Dona was in a state of shock. Her hair was falling out from where Angelo had pulled at it, and she felt the blood trickle down her cheek. She agreed.

Forced to call her father, she waited for him to pick her up. Once again, Dona felt like a disappointment, even though he didn't say a word.

The jury sentenced Angelo to six years for possession of an unauthorized firearm and attempted kidnapping. Since he was behind bars, he couldn't stop her from having the abortion, but she feared that he would never forget once he was out.

Dona didn't plan to date again anytime soon. Instead, she decided to pursue her dream and attend college. Wanting to learn more about human behavior, she majored in psychology at NYU so she could avoid making future mistakes with other men.

# Chapter 9 | Coffee Talk

### The Green Room

---

Joe's masked image appeared on the screen. He seemed to be in a rush.

"I have to go out for a while. Do you want anything before I leave?"

"Yes. I want to go home."

"All in good time. For now, can I bring you something?"

"I could use a cup of coffee."

"I'm fresh out, but I'm going to town for provisions. I'll pick some up for you. Would you like me to stop at McDonald's and get you a hamburger?"

"No, not really. I don't like fast food."

"Suit yourself."

The gravel crunched under his tires. Then— silence. For the first time since she'd been there, the room felt like it might let her breath. She realized it would be the perfect time to escape. *I need to pick the lock... something sharp.* She ran her finger along the prongs of the fork from the tray. *Useless!* The door was bolted from the outside.

Joe had been gone for hours. The minutes ran

together so slowly. She could have sworn the second hand on the clock was ticking backward. Finally, he was back. Dona tensed at the sound of crunching gravel as tires rolled over the driveway.

"Where have you been?" she shouted for him to appear on the screen.

He didn't.

Frustrated, she collapsed forward on the bed and beat the mattress with her fists until she had no strength left.

Loud music played in another room, George Thorogood's *One Bourbon, One Scotch, One Beer*. A familiar smell of marijuana seeped through the vents.

A tray slid through the slot, and she jumped up. Before she could get to the door, the hatch slammed, and the metal lock clamped shut, preventing her from voicing her anger.

Disgusted, she looked at the tray — another peanut butter and jelly sandwich. She wanted to kick herself for refusing the hamburger. Then she noticed a Styrofoam cup with steam curling from the top. Hot coffee! The first sip was warm and rich. It was just as she liked it, cream. No sugar. Forgetting the food, she took the coffee to the bed and sipped it slowly, allowing the steam to warm her cheeks. She savored the taste, yet a strange aftertaste lingered on her tongue.

The music blared again in the background. The clock told her it was ten. Despite the caffeine and the loud music, Dona's eyelids grew heavy. The music blurred. Something was wrong. A dizzy warmth settled over her. Crawling between the sheets, she succumbed to sleep. In her dreams, faces and memories rose up, pulling her back into the past.

*****

Dona tried to summon the memory of her early homemaker days, a blissful time before everything went wrong.

The time ticked by as she recalled the first time she met Richard. Impressionable and somewhat naïve, she was twenty-one when he swept her off her feet.

One Friday night, she went to a local dance club with her friends. The disco lights spun, and the music thumped against the walls like a heartbeat.

Dona looked stunning in her forest green halter jumpsuit. It came with a sheer jacket that covered her cleavage. She had developed before any of the girls in her elementary class and was always self-conscious. Wearing her hair straight and parted in the middle, she wrapped a headband across her forehead to complete her outfit.

The dance floor was crowded. Dona wanted to dance too, but her shyness stood in the way, so she just watched. While she chatted with her friends at the bar, a nice-looking man kept his eye on her. Her friends noticed and pointed out that she had an admirer.

Dona turned and smiled ever so slightly. She hadn't been admired in a long time. The attention felt strange ... but nice.

His dark hair was short and wavy, and his lean, long-legged physique reminded her of a long-distance runner.

Encouraged by her smile, he sauntered over to an empty stool next to her.

"Can I buy you a drink?" he asked over the thumping bass of the music.

The two engaged in a loud conversation. He introduced himself as Richard was from North Carolina. He told her he was an outdoor type and loved the woods and the mountains.

"How did you end up in New York?" she asked.

"Actually, the whole thing was a fluke. I had a layover in New York when I got out of the service. I wanted to see what all the hoopla was about. I don't care for crowds, but the city has plenty of wilderness preserves. The Founding Fathers got something right."

Richard's eyes wandered as they chatted. He glanced at an attractive woman as she passed by. *A wolf!* she thought. Dona knew the type, obsessed with the female form, and easily distracted by a pretty girl.

As the evening progressed, they discovered they didn't have much in common, but the conversation was easygoing. When the nightclub closed, it was time to say good night.

Richard wrapped his arms around her in a spontaneous hug and kissed her. "I'd like to see you again," he said.

"I just broke up with someone, and I'm not looking to jump into another relationship."

"I understand," he said. "We can take it slow and see where it leads us."

# Chapter 10 | Hanging Dog

## *Richard*

---

Dona wasn't sure she wanted to fall into another relationship soon after Angelo, but she gave Richard her number anyway.

Dona and Richard clicked almost immediately. They spent the fall hiking in the woods and enjoying the beauty of nature. As winter approached, they watched funny movies on television in her apartment. Richard was older and seemed to be in control of his life. His father owned a construction company. Hoping to retire, he persuaded Richard to return and take over the business.

One night, Richard took her hand during a movie and whispered, "Will you marry me?"

"What? But...."

"That's crazy, Richard. We've only known each other for a couple of months."

"I love you. I want to spend our lives together."

Dona had doubts. She didn't feel the same heady passion as he and wasn't sure she could keep up with him sexually. But she felt compelled to reciprocate whenever someone proclaimed their love for her. She recounted the men she thought she loved before him. It had never turned out well. She feared making the wrong decision. If she said no, she might change her mind. Was it her fear of being alone? It was typical of her to constantly second-guess herself. After giving it much thought, she accepted his proposal. At the time, she never thought she'd leave New York, but Richard had grown up in the country and was used to it.

They were married by the Justice of the Peace, and Dona packed her bags. She didn't want to leave her family, but she didn't want to live with her parents forever. Moving to another state with her husband made her feel independent.

Murphy, North Carolina, was a rural town with one supermarket, a post office, supply stores, and a few fast-food restaurants. Dona wasn't sure she'd be able to adjust to country life, but she was willing to give it a try.

Richard found some land on a ridge in a small rural community called Hanging Dog. The name wasn't as ominous as it sounded. It referred to an old American Indian legend. A brave man and his dog were tracking a deer that leaped across the creek. Hot on his trail, the dog jumped in after the deer and was swept away by the strong current. Luckily, he was caught on some branches and saved by the man. The Cherokees named the area Hanging Dog Creek.

Like a picture postcard, the lush, rolling hills with acres of woodland surrounding the town of Murphy. Little had changed over the years. Dona was impressed by the vivid sunsets on the ridgetop. But once the sun sank beyond the horizon, she shuddered at the vastness of the darkness. In the light of the moon, sets of eyes looked at her through the woods—raccoons, deer, mountain lions, and even an occasional black bear.

They stayed with Richard's parents until they could buy their own house, sleeping in the small, cramped room he had occupied as a child.

Six months later, they moved into their first home. She kept working, but Richard wanted her to be a homemaker. At first, she thought his motivations were to treat her like a princess, but she realized he had ulterior motives. He was concerned about her working with other men.

"Don't you trust me?"

"Of course, I do. I just don't trust other men."

When Dona became pregnant with their first child, the career issue was no longer up for debate. Richard Jr. was born in the dead of winter, during the Super Bowl, and with his birth, her professional dreams came to an end.

Dona could still hear the tree frogs at night and feel the stillness of the air. It took her a while to get used to a slower pace. She spent the first five years taking the role of wife and new mother seriously. At first, Dona didn't mind. She loved her house and playing the role of a Suzy Homemaker—cooking a full-course dinner with fresh ingredients every evening. She especially loved her Broilmaster propane gas barbecue. She grilled juicy steaks, melt-off-the-bone ribs, and tender chicken, but Richard would have been content with hot dogs and hamburgers.

Richard had a ravenous appetite—and a high libido. He wanted to make love every day. Dona always had a warning. He'd start by petting her legs or back, and then his hands would wander over her body. He always came up behind her in the kitchen and fondled her breasts. Sometimes it irritated her, and she felt as if he was groping.

"Please, stop!" Richard's sex drive was off the charts, while Dona's was all but gone. She wondered if he thought she was frigid. Since the birth of their son, she no longer felt any stirrings of the flesh.

Richard snuggled close to her in bed and put his hand on her breast. She pulled away.

"Please, Richard. I'm not in the mood. Can't you just lie next to me?"

"Ah, come on," he said.

"Is that all you ever think about?" Dona asked.

"I can't help it," he said. "I've always had a high libido."

"That's the problem. I DON'T! You're wearing me out."

# Chapter 11 | Kept Woman

## *Richard*

---

Once Richard left for work and Richie Jr. was on the school bus, she brewed a fresh pot of coffee. Dona had the house all to herself, just like her mother had done years ago when she was a homemaker. As a young girl, Dona had envisioned this lifestyle — a routine she had witnessed and somehow envied. The frustrations of life seemed more manageable when she was safe at home.

Being a city girl, Dona thought she would hate living in the country, but it wasn't as bad as she thought. There were plenty of trees, and the small town had little traffic. Still, she daydreamed of how her life would have been if she had stayed in New York. *Maybe I would have a high-paying job and live in a swanky apartment all my own.*

She missed New York, especially when she met her neighbors.

Dona recalled the first time she met them. They already knew each other well. One day, as she approached the bus stop, they were in deep conversation. The conversation stopped, and they both gaped at her. It made Dona feel uneasy, but she managed a smile.

"How do you like it here in North Carolina?" Ellen asked.

"So far, I like it."

"Do you work?" Tami asked.

"No, I'm a stay-at-home mom."

"Oh," Ellen said with a look of disdain.

It was an awkward moment, saved by the school bus lumbering down the street with its flashing red lights.

"Well, I have to go to work, and I don't want to be late," Ellen said.

"Me, too," Tami added.

As Dona turned to leave, she heard Tami whisper," Another Yankee!"

Ellen laughed. "No…. a damned Yankee. I don't think she's leaving."

That was almost eight years ago, and they never warmed up to her.

Dona slipped into her jeans and one of Richard's T-shirts to work on her garden before the noonday sun.

Dona took pride in her garden. The faint scent of honeysuckle floated through her open windows in May. Richard had laughed at her attempts to train the vines upward along the hillside, but Dona stubbornly pointed the stems upward until the whole hill was lush with growth. Although she didn't have a green thumb, she started a vegetable patch and cultivated flowering plants in full view of her kitchen windows. She lined the edge of the woods with mature clippings of yellow forsythias she had lovingly nourished, then watched as the seedlings grew larger every year. She waited impatiently for the cherry blossoms to burst into vibrant pink each spring. She would have a full harvest by summer if there weren't a sudden drop in temperature or if the birds didn't eat them all.

Still early, there was dew on the grass. The air smelled clean and heavy with the scent of flowers. Surrounded by her garden, nothing else existed. Dogwood flowers bloomed in white and pink, and the forsythia was vibrant with yellow buds. She planted hibiscus, her favorite flower, in white, pink, yellow, red, and peach. Each color had a significant meaning. Red, traditionally worn by Tahitian women behind their ears, signified that they were available for marriage.

The weather in Murphy had moved well beyond uncomfortable. It was almost one hundred degrees by midday, sending humidity to oppressive levels as thunderstorms hammered the town.

The hiss of air brakes from the bus down the street snapped her out of her daydreams. She rushed to take the cookies out of the oven.

Richie burst through the front door. "I'm home!" he announced. "I smell cookies!" He threw off his backpack and scrambled up on the kitchen stool.

They had a ritual. First, Richie told Dona about his day at school, and then she helped him with his homework.

Dona poured a glass of milk.

"What's wrong, Richie? You look upset."

"Nothing!"

"You can tell me."

"Well, Lily's mom says you're a kept woman," he whispered.

Dona frowned. "Why does Lily say that?"

"Because you don't work."

"I do work. I work in the house."

"But you don't have a *real job*, like Lily's mom."

"Lily isn't home right now, is she?"

"No, she goes to the after-school program."

"Is that where you'd like to go after school?"

"No," Richie cried. "I want to come home."

"What else does Lily's mom say?"

"She says that you're not dependent."

"Do you mean independent?"

"Uh-huh. Yeah. What's that?"

"Independent is not relying on someone else to care for you."

"Do you rely on Daddy?" he asked.

"Yeah, I guess so." Dona suddenly felt small in his gaze. She stretched a piece of Saran Wrap over the remaining cookies.

"Why don't you go out and play? We'll do the homework later."

Kept woman. The comment struck a nerve.

Her dream was to be independent. Things just didn't turn out that way.

While Richie played outside, she picked up the phone. She needed to hear a voice that wouldn't judge her.

"Hi, Mom. I feel so down. Richie just asked me

why I don't work. He thinks I should have a regular job. Maybe he's right."

"Maybe you should find a part-time job while he's at school," she suggested.

"What kind of job could I get? I never finished college."

"They're always looking for substitute teachers. Maybe you can get a job at the school."

"That's a great idea, Mom. They're building a new elementary school. It's due to open next fall, and I'm sure they'll be hiring. It would get me out of the house, and I'd be home in time for Richie."

And so, Dona applied.

# Chapter 12 | J-E-L-L-O

*Richard*

---

The summer flew by, and there was no news from the school board. She was about to give up when a letter arrived from the Department of Education. Her hands trembled as she tore open the envelope. One line was enough to crush the hope she'd carried all summer.

"We regret to inform you that, at this time, we do not have any open positions for substitute teaching."

Her heart sank, but she read on.

"There is a position in the cafeteria if you are interested. Please call and schedule an interview."

Dona crushed the letter, tossed it in the trash, and then called her mother.

"I didn't get the job, Mom. I guess I wasn't qualified. Instead, they offered me a position in the cafeteria."

"Why don't you take it?"

"I don't want to work in a lunchroom. Cafeteria women are so matronly."

"Oh, Dona. Get your foot in the door. Once you're in, maybe you can ask for a transfer."

"Hmm. Maybe you're right, Mom. Thanks."

*****

The lunchroom supervisor was a no-nonsense, southern woman, Dona judged to be in her late fifties. She allowed no informality and insisted that she be called Mrs. Waldron.

"We have stringent rules here," she said. "Everyone has to wear a hairnet on the line."

*Ugh, a hairnet. How degrading*! She tucked her hair under the black web.

"This is not a fashion show," Mrs. Waldron said as if she were reading her mind. "Do you have a problem with that?"

"No, ma'am." *Did I say, ma'am?*

Dona was suddenly transported back to her childhood. That same humiliating feeling she had felt years ago when Mrs. Beck, her math teacher, called her to the chalkboard to solve an equation. Dona could feel her staring as she stood helpless with the chalk in her hand, held mid-air but not touching the board.

"That's what you get when you don't do your homework," she said. "Go back to your seat."

Mrs. Waldron stood up, pulling Dona back to the present.

"Come with me, and I'll show you the kitchen."

Dona followed her to the back. Mrs. Waldron handed her a scouring pad and told her to start by scrubbing the pots. The smell of meatloaf turned her stomach, and the heat from the ovens made her feel like she was in a sauna. When she thought she would pass out, Mrs. Waldron's voice rang out from the kitchen.

"Dona, I need you on the Jell-O station."

Glad to escape the pots, she put on a white apron and tied it around her waist.

The cafeteria came alive with a never-ending parade of laughing children. Some lined up to get a hot lunch; others went through the milk line and then sat at their assigned tables with brown bags from home. As the third graders filed in, Dona looked out at the sea of bobbing heads, searching for Richie. She waved as he joined his friends at their table. He always brought his lunch to school. He preferred food from home, partly because of the surprise and funny notes she put in his lunchbox.

"Look! It's Richie's mom," a boy shouted as the fifth graders made their way through the line.

Dona recognized the kid from Richie's class, but the line moved so quickly that she couldn't stop working to look for her son. As a bead of sweat escaped her hairnet, Dona heard a familiar voice.

"Hi, Dona," Ellen said in her sing-song voice.

When she looked up, she spotted Ellen and Tami, in crisp skirt suits, every hair in place.

"What are you doing here?" Dona asked, trying to hold a smile.

"We started working today as substitute teachers," Tami said with a sardonic grin.

"Substitute teachers?"

Dona felt her face turn red, like the Jell-O that had run down her apron. She wanted to disappear under the counter. The line of children backed up, and Mrs. Waldron yelled for her to speed it up.

It kept moving but seemed to go on forever. When the last class came through, Dona cleaned her station and returned to scrubbing more pots, hoping that no one noticed her tears as they mixed with the steam from the hot water. Her self-esteem sank to an all-time low. She looked up to see Mrs. Waldron's stern face searing into her like a hot iron.

"Did I do something wrong?"

"What happened to you?"

"Huh, what do you mean?"

"Upfront on the serving line. Who were those two women who came through?"

"Oh, them. They're my neighbors."

"I take it they're not friends."

"No, not really. I told them I had applied for a substitute position. I didn't get it, but they did."

"So, now you feel embarrassed to be working in a cafeteria. By the look on your face, it didn't take a genius to understand.

"I don't know why I moved to North Carolina. I just don't fit in."

"Gibberish," she said, her eyes darkening. "Those bitches are jealous. They see you as a threat."

"A threat?"

"Of course. You're in the South, darlin'—not exactly the place for high fashion or any of that there intellectual stuff. You're a city girl moving into their territory, darlin'. They want to prove they're as good as you."

"But I'm not like that. I didn't even finish college."
She shook her head at Dona's naiveté.

"Unfortunately, women can be very judgmental. They mistake your kindness for weakness. You need confidence."

Dona thought she spotted a slight smile on Mrs. Waldron's lips.

"You seem like a good girl, Dona. Don't let people manipulate your emotions."

After scrubbing the last pot, she put her apron in the laundry pile and gave Mrs. Waldron her notice.

Dona only lasted one day as a cafeteria lady, but she straightened her posture and held her head high with renewed confidence.

That night, instead of crying, she filled out a college application. For the first time in years, the shame in her chest had somewhere to go—forward.

The next day, she enrolled at the community college. The other students were much younger and seemed to breeze through their courses. Dona had a hard time juggling home life with school. It felt like crawling through broken glass at times, but she persevered. Her tenacity wouldn't allow her to quit, and she proudly displayed her bachelor's degree in Psychotherapy.

After graduating, a new stage of her life began to take shape.

Against Richard's wishes, she took a job as an apprentice for a private psychiatrist in town. The best part of her day was being at work. It was a challenge figuring out the complexities of the patients. Most had trust issues, and Dona was good at making them feel at ease. With clients, she could be patient and understanding. Each new patient had a reason for staying with an abusive partner. She could relate to their emotional pain but distanced herself from her own.

Dona wasn't happy, but she felt safe. That all ended after 9-11. Richard seemed to regress into his Vietnam days. Dona never questioned his experiences. She assumed he had come out unscathed, but he seemed to change overnight. Now, they surfaced. He bought a motorcycle and spent his time in the garage.

The man she'd built a life with started to disappear beneath the haze of smoke and sixties music. He even started growing pot among the tomatoes — as if she wouldn't notice. He claimed a little weed helped him unwind.

He liked to watch television when he wasn't riding his bike or puttering in the garage. To Dona, it was a mindless activity. It was vital for her to be productive. She was always busy running the household and maintaining her fitness. Her idea of leisure was taking long evening walks or riding her bike. She rarely wanted to watch television except at night when it gleamed in the darkened living room. They stared at it, nothing to say. He lit a marijuana roach and sucked on the tip. The ember glowed, and tiny sparks flicked onto the carpet.

"Do you have to do that in the house?" she complained.

"You don't know how to relax," Richard said.

"Maybe you should have a toke."

An early riser, Dona didn't like to stay up too late. Richard, on the other hand, was a night owl. He stayed up long after she went to bed. She heard him banging around in the kitchen and pulled the pillow over her head.

Dona's eyes opened in the middle of the night, hearing the drone of the television in the living room. Her hunch was that he had fallen asleep with the television blaring. Irritated, she had to go and retrieve him.

After an hour, his body heat had her throwing the covers off and scrambling for the edge of the bed. She'd turn on the overhead fan and try to fall back asleep. Within an hour, night sweats soaked her side of the bed. She opened her eyes and realized the fan was off. Dona turned it on again.

"I just shut that," Richard mumbled.

"I can't sleep without a fan."

It then took her a long time to fall asleep, and she woke to find the fan off. Again.

On, off, on, off. They played this game every night.

"We're not sleep-compatible," she'd complain.

Even though she and Richard had problems in their marriage, they weren't bad enough to make her want to leave.

# Chapter 13 | Tick-Tock

## The Green Room

---

Dona's ankles healed, but her days of captivity dragged on until she lost count. Her world had shrunk to the four walls in which she was trapped. She had the small clock by her bed, but she couldn't tell if it was a.m. or p.m. Only the meals supplied through the slot in the door gave her a clue. Surely he wouldn't serve her oatmeal at six o'clock at night. It looked like mush. She left it on the tray and drank the coffee. Since she had requested it, he included it with breakfast every morning. Sometimes it was cold, but she drank it anyway.

Time blurred into oatmeal and coffee. Tick. Tock. Tick. Tock.

Joe didn't make his morning appearance on the computer. Dona's eyes darted to the door and then to the floor, expecting her breakfast tray. She waited for him to appear, but the screen remained black. *He's obviously angry and must be punishing me.* She recalled something her professor had said in a psychology class. "Psychopaths can't handle confrontation."

She didn't hear any sounds in the house. *Maybe he isn't home. What if he doesn't return?* No one knew she was there. No one would bring her food. She imagined herself as a lifeless skeleton and had an anxiety attack, hyperventilating until tears streamed down her face. Green—the color was supposed to have relaxing qualities, but it didn't ease her anxiety.

Continuously checking the clock, four hours went by. Her stomach grumbled with hunger. She didn't hear his car pull up, so she was taken aback when his image popped up on the screen.

"Did you miss me?"

"Where have you been?"

"Sorry about that. I had a busy day."

"What if something happened to you? I would have died of starvation."

"You're so negative. Calm down."

His words clawed at old wounds. Dona hated it when someone accused her of being negative. Richard always used it to make her unsure. It had a way of making her unravel. She had to keep her lips tight, fearing curse words would spew out. Control always wore the same face.

"I'll calm down, but I haven't eaten all day. I'm starving."

"Yes, I'm sure. You'll get food. First things first. You never answered my question the other day."

She fought to rein in her anxiety and keep a poker face. "Which question was that?"

"What do you want in a man?"

"Why does that matter to you?"

"I'm trying to understand what you wanted in your life."

"Fine. If I answer, will you bring me some food?"

"Yes."

"I want a man without a hidden agenda. Someone who loves me enough not to control me."

"And what do you offer in exchange for this devotion?"

"Mutual love and respect."

"If that were true, you wouldn't have thrown away the men who did love you. Is it because they didn't have money?"

"I don't care about money."

"You're not being honest with me."

She waited for his explanation, but he was calculated in his silence. "I know you!" he finally murmured.

"What do you know?"

"You're one of those women who expect your man to work all day, then come home and help with chores they didn't get to between soap operas."

"That's ridiculous. Women help men all the time. They pick up the slack so men can work their jobs. What's wrong with a little reverse support?"

"Women are selfish. They expect men to work and provide them with money."

She sighed. "Of course, I like money, but that's not what motivates me."

"So, is it the things money can buy that motivates you?"

"Money is required to live. Some men are better

providers than others. The problem is that I pick men who think too small."

The screen turned black. I guess I pissed him off again.

Joe was wrong about one thing. Dona had the drive to achieve—to better her life. She didn't care about being rich.

He had said he'd give her food, and now she wondered if he would keep his promise. Her mind drifted back to Richard and the business he inherited from his father. She did the office work while he was out in the field. Dona had high hopes that they would be successful.

*Leafers* came every fall to enjoy the vibrant foliage and appreciate the serene natural environment. Many decided to sell their homes and relocate to North Carolina, leading to a housing shortage. The town had grown, tourists had come, and he let it all slip away between beer cans and joints.

The business never did bloom. His workers lost respect for him and went out on their own.

The smell of barbecue wafted through the cracks in the door. Dona kept her eyes glued to the slot, waiting for it to open. An hour went by, and her hunger grew along with her anger.

Finally, she heard him approach. The tray came through the slot. She rushed over to the food: a piece of chicken and a potato. Grateful it wasn't another peanut butter sandwich, she bit into the chicken thigh. Dona loved the dark meat and relished the grilled taste.

While married, she enjoyed food cooked on the grill and thought she was quite skilled at it. Even though she didn't want the potato, she wrapped it in a napkin, just in case he decided to withhold breakfast. There was a bottle of water on the tray, but she drank the coffee instead. Lately, Joe had started including coffee with dinner. It was a routine she was used to from her days as a homemaker. After every meal, she and Richard would sit outside on the patio and drink a cup of coffee.

The tick-tock of the clock grated on her nerves. She resisted the urge to pull the plug. *How would I know the time? Does it matter?* She felt the same way during her marriage to Richard — numb.

Tick, tock, tick, tock, the sound faded as her eyes grew heavy.

*****

Dona woke up but didn't feel the mattress's softness. Instead, the coldness of concrete seeped into her bones. She stared up at the once familiar lightbulb hanging from the beam. Horrified, she sat up. *I'm back in the basement.* It took her a few minutes to recall how angry Joe had been when she insulted his intelligence. Pain jolted her back to reality. She ran to the door and pounded it with her fists.

"Let me out of here," she screamed. There was no response. She could hear Joe walking above her as the floorboards creaked. Small particles of dust floated down from the ceiling.

"I'm sorry!"

This time, there was no pillow. No blanket. Just cold concrete. Shivering, she curled up to keep warm. Every muscle in her body hurt, and her skin was numb.

She searched her arsenal of knowledge about psychopaths and narcissists. It was all about them. She had to use that to appeal to him.

Without the pesky clock she hated, Dona had no way to keep track of time. She didn't know if hours or days had gone by.

"Joe," she shouted, sure he could hear her in the underground tomb. "If you leave me down here to die, all your questions will go unanswered. Everything you've done will have been for nothing. It's a shame because I was starting to enjoy our conversations."

Her plan didn't seem to be working. Freezing, she drifted in and out of consciousness but welcomed the relief from her suffering as she sank into darkness.

*Why doesn't he just kill me?*

When she opened her eyes, she saw the tray. Anticipating a sandwich, she rushed toward it. All she saw were crackers and orange juice. *I guess this is his version of bread and water.*

The orange juice was sweet—too sweet. But she drank it anyway. If this was her ticket out of the dungeon, so be it. Like Alice in Wonderland, she chugged it down, and soon the drug crept through her veins.

As a thin black shadow approached her, Dona struggled to pull herself back to reality, but she couldn't force her eyes to remain open.

# Chapter 14 | Honeysuckle

## *Richard*

---

Dona heard the distant chirping of birds. They made her think of home. For a moment, she forgot where she was. She opened her eyes. The green walls closed in again, as if mocking her.

"Good morning," Joe said. "It's about time you're up. It's a beautiful day. It's not like you to sleep your life away. I know how much you enjoy being productive. You have a lot of things to work out."

"You left me to die in the basement."

"It was for your own good. Clear your head — get your priorities straight."

"Priorities?"

"Yes, you know — love, relationships — that kind of stuff."

"I don't want to talk about that. I'm hungry."

"I'll get you something to eat, but after, I expect you to talk to me."

"I'll answer anything you ask. Just bring me food."

"Coming right up. Maybe you should take a shower, though. You're looking pretty rough."

Dona went to the bathroom and looked at herself

in the mirror. Her once-satin olive complexion was now blotchy and raw. She turned the shower water to extra hot and let it run over her body until her skin prickled like needles. It was the only way she could get warm.

She came out of the bathroom to find the breakfast tray waiting. Clean, warm, and with a full stomach, she began to feel a little better. The peanut butter tasted good this time, and she wished for more.

Joe gave her another hour before he popped on the screen.

"Are you ready to talk about love?"

"Love is fleeting, and relationships are a landmine."

"Relationships are a contract between two people."

"Yes, and one that men seem to break whenever something better comes along."

"So, you believe in monogamy!"

"That is part of a marriage contract, isn't it?"

"True, as long as the woman meets her end of the bargain."

"What do you mean by that?"

"Well, when a man is in a romantic relationship with a woman, he expects to have his needs met. If she breaks that contract, he'll probably turn to infidelity."

"That's insulting," she snapped. "Women aren't just sex objects."

Joe laughed. "Women use their sexuality all the time," he shot back. "They hold all the power and then expect men to be faithful."

"How dare you! Most women just want to feel safe and loved. Sex starts in the brain. A man can't expect a woman to ignore things that happen outside of the bedroom. It goes both ways... a woman can have an affair if she doesn't get her needs met, just as easily as a man."

Click! The screen went black. Her chest tightened. Breath came in short bursts. The clock on the nightstand ticked louder and louder. She gripped the edge of the bed until her fingers ached. She recalled the first time she experienced a panic attack. It was the day things went wrong with her marriage. The memory stuck in her throat like a lump.

While cleaning the den, Dona noticed Richard's laptop was open. Since she didn't need a passcode, she scrolled through some of his emails. Unsure of what she was looking for, her eyes landed on one particular email. It was from a woman. *honeysuckle@gmail.com*.

The subject line stole her breath. *I miss you inside of me*. Her hand hovered over the mouse. One click.

Richard. Thank you for a wonderful dinner and a lovely night together. When can we get together again?

With an uneasy pit in her stomach, she realized that her husband was cheating on her. She reread the email, torturing herself with her new reality—an unfaithful husband.

Although they were now divorced, that was the day their marriage ended.

Aware of his deception, Dona noticed things she usually would have ignored. The nights he came home late from work or the times when she called, and his phone went directly to voicemail.

She glanced at the clock. Richard was two hours late. Hearing the garage door open, she dabbed her eyes with a tissue and set the table for dinner.

Richard came up behind her and gave her a peck on the cheek.

"Sorry, I'm late. I had a difficult client."

Yeah, I bet!

Richard complimented her cooking, saying no one could grill a steak as well as she. He grabbed the silverware, going out of his way to be helpful. His eyes fluttered as he cut a piece of meat and shoved it into his mouth.

Dona waited for the proverbial *other shoe* to drop.

"The weather has been nice," he said. "I think we'll have an early fall."

"The leaves will be brilliant up in the mountains for our trip next week."

"Yeah. I meant to tell you. Some guys are going on a bike ride along the Blue Ridge next weekend. I was thinking about joining them."

"What about our plans in Cherokee?"

"We go there every year. I'd like to do something different."

"Oh."

Disappointment washed over her.

"Don't give me that face."

"I'm just a little surprised. You've never wanted to spend time with friends. Besides, I was looking forward to getting away."

"Can't we reschedule our trip? We can book into

that lodge you've wanted to stay at."

"Yes, that might be fun."

Dona cleared off the table. Having barely touched her food, she tossed it in the garbage disposal.

Suspicion fogged her mind. *He's using the bike trip to steal away for the weekend. Maybe the guys were really honeysuckle. Should I confront him?* There would be no alternative but to go to the divorce court. She decided it would be best not to say a word. She swallowed the resentment whole. But resentment had sharp edges. It cut on the way down.

# Chapter 15 | Gander

## *Austin*

---

As Richie Jr. got older and more independent, Dona had more free time during the day, so she joined a fitness gym. She met a good-looking man at the juice bar the first week there, with muscular shoulders and light brown hair bleached by the sun.

"Hi, I'm Austin Braun," he said, lowering his Serengeti sunglasses. "Are you new here? I don't remember seeing you before."

"Yes, I just joined."

"I've been coming here for over two years. If you like, I can show you how to use the Nautilus equipment."

"That would be great! Maybe you can show me which machine is good for toning the arms."

"Sure."

He led her to one of the machines and demonstrated its operation. "This will tone your triceps, and the machine next to it will work on your biceps."

Dona set the weights and sat to do a few repetitions.

"Where're you from?" Austin asked.

"New York."

"I thought so. I love the accent."

"My husband grew up in this area. I'm still adjusting to it. What about you?"

"I'm from a small town in Kansas, a real country boy."

Dona finished, sliding over to the next piece of equipment. She rubbed her arms. "I think I feel it working already."

Austin took her place and moved the setting to a higher weight. Sweat glued his shirt to his back, and beads of sweat lined his forehead.

"Whew! I sure can use something cold to drink. Let's go to the juice bar. We can get some protein smoothies."

"I'm not sure about smoothies, but I could use some cold water."

They walked to the concession area.

"You must find North Carolina a big change from New York," he said.

"You're telling me!"

Dona finished the water, and they fell into an awkward silence.

"I think I'm finished today," Austin said. "I have to get to work."

"What do you do?"

"I'm a satellite technician."

"For NASA?"

Austin laughed. "No, for the cable company."

"Oh," she said, feeling foolish. "Thank you for

showing me the equipment."

"Will you be here tomorrow?" Austin asked.

"I should be. I've been trying to come every morning. Today I got a late start."

"I'm glad. Otherwise, I wouldn't have met you. Maybe we could work out together."

Before he left, Austin turned to her. "Welcome to Murphy, city girl. Don't let them change you."

"I won't!" Dona laughed.

The next day, Dona put on a little makeup before going to the gym.

"Hi, Dona," she heard Austin say.

Her heart rate increased as he approached.

"I've been thinking about you," he said.

"Really?"

"Yeah. I missed hearing your New York accent."

Dona blushed.

"Let's get started," he said, and they made their way around the gym. She enjoyed his attention. It was a lovely way to spend the morning. When they finished the last workout, she couldn't believe how quickly time had passed.

"What do you say we go for a little lunch?"

"I don't know."

"Oh, come on. I promise not to bite."

"You know, I'm married," she reminded him.

"There's no harm in eating together, is there?"

"No, I don't think so."

"Okay, then. I know of a great place for burgers. Would you like to go?"

"Yes, I'd love it."

"I'll meet you out front after we shower," Austin said. "We'll take my car."

Dona nodded and headed for the women's locker room. As she washed the sweat from her workout off, her nerves were frayed. She had been afraid it would come to this. She tried to steady her breathing. Exhilarated by the prospect of a forbidden liaison, her body trembled with excitement. There's still time, she reasoned — time to call the whole thing off.

Richard's cheating email flashed into her mind. *Honeysuckle! What's good for the goose!*

Austin was waiting for her outside. Dressed in jeans and a button-down shirt, he looked rugged, like a cowboy, but there was a sweetness in his eyes that reached out to her. It was impossible to resist his smooth, charming personality. Her stomach fluttered as she slid into the passenger seat of his car.

"We're just two friends having lunch," she reminded him … or herself.

At the restaurant, the waitress came to their table immediately. "Can I take your order?"

"I'll have a burger."

"I'll have the same," Dona said.

"So, what made you leave Kansas?" she asked.

"It was time, I guess. Satellite television was becoming popular. They needed someone to travel. I was free…so why not?"

"Is it different there?"

"No, it's a typical small town."

"I don't like small towns," she said. "Everyone seems to know your business."

Austin's smile lingered across the table. Dona wrapped her hands around her water glass, the condensation cool against her fingers. It felt both safe and dangerous to be with him. She hadn't felt that flirty in years.

The waitress set their plates in front of them. "Is there anything else I can get for you?" she asked.

"No," they both said at the same time. When she left, they continued their conversation.

"Are you Italian?" Austin asked.

"Yes, how did you know?"

"It's those big brown eyes," he teased.

She noticed that his eyes were blue. "I've never gone out with someone who has blue eyes," she said.

Austin laughed. "I'm glad that I'm the first."

They sat for an hour, talking and laughing. Dona enjoyed every moment, happy that she had decided to have lunch with him. She felt a connection as if she'd known him all her life. Being with Austin seemed natural, yet she felt a sense of guilt.

"I should leave soon."

"Already?" he said with disappointment. "All right, but you have to promise."

"Promise what?"

"Promise that you'll have lunch with me again."

She smiled.

He drove her back to the gym.

"I'll see you tomorrow," he said.

The next day, she couldn't wait to see Austin. The budding relationship made it harder to concentrate on working out. Their daily workouts seemed so innocent. She convinced herself she wasn't doing anything wrong.

Richie was getting picked up for a playdate with a classmate, so she wasn't in a rush. Austin walked Dona to her car. The parking lot felt bright, the sun gleaming into her eyes. Fumbling for the keys, she opened the door. Austin reached for her, and she let him pull her close. Their bodies came together, and she savored his warm lips as they kissed.

"Follow me back to my apartment," he whispered.

Something inside of her yearned for his love. In her heart, she knew if she were alone with him, the temptation would be too much for her to resist, but she didn't want to go home. Not yet.

"Okay, but I have to get home by dinnertime." "Great. You can follow me in your car."

Dona looked around the parking lot to see if anyone was watching. For once, she was thankful she didn't know anyone in town. She could still say no. She could drive home, make dinner, and pretend nothing had ever happened. But she waited for him to pull out of the parking spot and trailed behind him. Along the way, she tried to justify her actions. Richard was having an affair. She'd known it for months.

Austin made a left at the light. Soon, they were at his apartment complex. He turned in and punched the code for his gate. She followed his car around the building and parked in front of his apartment.

"Come on," he said. "I have roommates, but they're at work."

Dona felt like a naughty teenager. It was the same

feeling she had when she used to cut school. Austin opened the door and held it for her to enter. The faint smell of detergent mingled with a musky scent of masculinity.

"How many guys live here?" she asked.

"There used to be four of us." He sat on the couch and motioned for her to sit next to him. "But my friend Seth went back home."

Worried that his roommates might come home early, Dona fidgeted on the couch. She crossed her legs, picked up one of the throw pillows, and held it on her lap for security. She felt like a teenager, skipping school. *I shouldn't be here*, she thought.

Austin's hand brushed against hers, and the rest of her resolve slipped away. They shared a long, soft kiss. He stood up, took her hand, and led her through the hall, past his friends' rooms, and into his. It was light outside, but he lit a candle beside his bed and unbuttoned his shirt.

"Do you have protection?" she asked as he held her in his embrace.

"No, but we can be careful."

Dona froze. "I can't get pregnant. Maybe we should wait."

"I understand," he said, reaching for his shirt.

"Wait!"

Austin turned and kissed her again, and Dona gave in to her desire. Soft light created shadows on the wall as they made love. It was like a dream—like slipping into someone else's life. Time seemed to stand still, and she wasn't sure how long she was there.

# Chapter 16 | Bundle of Joy

### *Richard*

---

In Austin's apartment, they were a couple. After a brief greeting, Dona and Austin would retreat to his room and lock the door. Oblivious to everything happening down the hall, his roommates sat in the living room, drinking beer and watching ESPN. Austin put a record on the stereo, and the music drowned out their voices. No one else existed except the two of them. After a while, it became harder for them to separate.

"It's getting late," she said.

"I wish you could stay the night," he complained.

"What would I tell Richard?"

"I don't know. Think of something."

"Don't go," he pleaded and kissed her again.

"I have to," she insisted, jumping out of bed to search for her clothes.

"Don't leave," he insisted, pulling her back as she tried to slip away.

"I have no choice!"

"You do have a choice. You could leave Richard and marry me. I'm tired of sneaking around and hiding our love."

Dona had no intention of leaving her marriage, especially with Richie. She could see the discontent in his eyes.

"Maybe we shouldn't see each other anymore," he said.

"You could be right," she agreed. But she sensed that he was only bluffing.

Austin walked her to the car. "Can I see you tomorrow?"

"We'll see." She smiled and they kissed.

Dona accelerated as soon as he disappeared in her rearview mirror.

She thought she loved Austin, but if that were true, why didn't she want to be with him? *Am I really in love with him, or is it only lust?*

On the way home, her mind kept drifting to Austin. Distracted, she drove onto their street without thinking about what she would say if Richard were already home. Trees obstructed her view, so she couldn't see the house until she pulled up front. Her breath caught in her throat when she saw his truck in the driveway.

"Where were you all day?" Richard asked.

Dona felt her face turn red. "I went to the gym and had a late dental appointment. You're home early."

She sensed he was suspicious, but their conversation was cut short by the school bus.

"Why didn't you pick up Richie from school?"

"He wanted to ride the bus home today."

Dona rushed out the front door. Her explanation seemed to satisfy him for the moment.

Feeling as though she evened the score, she had put his betrayal behind her.

Austin wouldn't leave her alone. She knew she should have managed the situation better. In the end, she had no choice but to cancel her gym membership.

That night, they made love for the first time in months. Dona focused on saving her marriage and initiating sex more often. Richard agreed to her request for date night. She let Richie Jr. stay at his friend's house every Friday after school, and reciprocated by having Jeremy spend the night on Saturday. She cooked all Richard's favorite meals and gave him her full attention when he told her stories about his day. Things seemed to get better between them for a while. He came home from work on time and even finished projects around the house.

*****

Six weeks later, Dona's breasts seemed larger, and her shirt felt fuller. Her period was late. *Is it possible that I'm pregnant? Maybe it's Richard's.*

The next day, Richie woke up with a fever and felt too unwell to attend school. Dona called the doctor and made an appointment for that afternoon. Since she was already going to be at the doctor's, Dona asked about a pregnancy test.

"Come on back. We'll get a urine sample," the nurse said.

After the test, she led Dona to the examination room with Richie. "The doctor will be in soon."

Dr. Hamilton examined Richie. She looked in his ears and swabbed the back of his throat.

"Richie has strep throat. I'll give you a prescription for amoxicillin, and he'll be fine."

"As for you, my dear…." She turned toward Dona and smiled. "Congratulations. You're expecting."

"What?" Dona felt a bit woozy and clutched the sides of the exam table to steady herself. "Oh no, I can't be!"

Dr. Hamilton's smile disappeared. "I'll give you a referral to the Women's clinic." She scribbled something on a pad. "I'm also prescribing something for your nausea and a prenatal vitamin."

Dona left the office in a daze and stopped at the drugstore to fill the prescriptions. An elderly woman noticed the pharmacist counting out the pink prenatal pills. She placed them in a container with the image of a smiling child.

"Bless your heart," she said. "You must be pregnant."

"They're not for me," Dona denied and tucked the pills into her purse.

When she arrived home, she went into the kitchen for soda crackers to settle her stomach. Feeling a little better, she thought about Austin. *Maybe our love is not over.* She dialed his number.

"The number you dialed is disconnected," the message said.

Disconnected?

As soon as Richard came home, Dona made an excuse to leave.

"I have to pick something up at the supermarket," she told him.

On the way to Austin's apartment, she tried to imagine what his child would be like. He was going to be a father. *He has to know!* Dona knew he'd insist she leave Richard. *Maybe I should!*

Austin's car wasn't in the parking lot. Something didn't feel right. She knocked on the door and held her breath. A strange man answered. The place looked different... smelled different. Even before the man said she had the wrong address, she realized—Austin was gone. *Perhaps he went back to Kansas.* She never thought to ask what town he lived in. Now there would be no way to tell him about the baby and no hope of finding a better solution.

The next day, Dona dialed the number Dr. Hamilton had given her. She waited, listening to the recording: "Are you pregnant and confused? We may be able to help." She took a deep breath.

"Fairborn Women's Clinic, can I help you?"

"Yes, I... I need to make an appointment for an abortion as soon as possible."

"We can get you in tomorrow to talk with a counselor."

"I don't need a counselor. I need an abortion."

"The doctor only performs those procedures on Mondays. You'll need to be here by 6:00 a.m. Don't eat or drink anything after midnight."

"Thank you." She hung up and had a good cry.

# Chapter 17 | Excuses

The following week, Richie had recovered from his strep throat. After dropping him off at school, she drove to the Clinic, which was almost thirty miles away. Dona wasn't happy about it, but he might fight her for custody of their son if Richard found out, and she couldn't risk losing Richie. Suppressing her guilt, she vowed never to have an affair again.

Nevertheless, that didn't help her now. She wanted to turn the car around and go home. She stopped at a red light, envisioning what the child inside of her might look like. Maybe it would have Austin's blue eyes or his blond hair.

She was already ten minutes late when she approached the clinic.

In front of the building, protesters stood with signs hung around their necks, repeatedly chanting, "Stop abortion now," as they walked in a circle. Suddenly, a man jumped out in front of her car. Dona had to slam on the brakes to avoid hitting him. He carried a sign that read, "Don't murder innocent babies." *Of all the days to have a protest. Why today?* Her hands gripped the steering wheel as she searched for an open spot, parking away from the crowd. An officer was present to maintain the protest's peacefulness. He escorted her to the side entrance.

She signed in and took a seat in the waiting area. A nurse opened the door and called her name. Dona followed her to a room in the back with an examining table and a large overhead light fixture. She handed her a faded green gown.

"Take your clothes off in the bathroom. You can keep your socks on. I'll leave this blanket for you to cover yourself."

The nurse left. Dona locked the bathroom door with trembling hands. Her fingers played with the top button of her shirt as she debated whether to keep her baby.

Still unsure about what to do, she came out and climbed onto the table. It seemed like she lay there for a long time. Dona was losing her nerve. *I can't do this!* She was about to get up and leave when the doctor came into the room.

"Hi, I'm Doctor Zuckerman."

She gave him a weak smile.

"I know you're nervous, but try to relax. This won't take long."

Listening to the doctor as he gave instructions to the nurse, her mind raced. It's too late, she thought. The doctor would think she was a nutcase if she jumped off the table now. He turned on the overhead light, making Dona blink and close her eyes. She recalled something she had read in a book once. *It takes more courage to save a life than to take one.*

"Okay, I think we're ready," Doctor Zuckerman said. He put her legs in the stirrups and lifted the gown.

The room was spinning. Dona suddenly felt sick.

"Stop!" she screamed.

"What's wrong?"

"I can't!" she cried. Dona grabbed her clothes and slipped into the bathroom. She ripped off the gown, wriggled into her jeans, and pulled on her shirt.

She ran past the medical staff in the front office without a word. She stepped outside, expecting the protesters, but they were gone.

Once in her car, Dona sighed with relief.

Dona stared at the bag lying on the passenger seat all the way home. *I'll have to ditch it in the next trash can at the gas station.* With relief and panic, Dona realized that her problem had remained. She was glad she hadn't gone through with it, but now she had to figure out how to tell Richard they were having a baby.

Still shaky, she drove to pick up Richie. He was standing with his friend Jeremy and his mother.

They ran up to Dona.

"Can Richie come to my house and play?" Jeremy asked.

"I don't know. That's up to your mother."

Susan smiled. "We've promised the boys a play date for months. Tomorrow is Saturday. I'm off work and thought I could take them to the zoo. We would love to have Richie spend the night if that's all right with you."

"Please, Mommy!" Richie begged.

"Well, all right, but you'll need your pajamas."

"He can wear a pair of Jeromy's. It's no problem. I'll bring him home in the afternoon. I have your phone number and address in my notepad."

"All right, but you had better give me yours, just in case."

"Great." Susan jotted down her number. I'll call you.

Dona kissed Richie goodbye and drove home. Along the way, she stopped at the supermarket. Richard came home to a three-course dinner and a bottle of wine.

Dona didn't see the hammer Richard left by the front door as she stepped inside. Blood streamed from her foot onto the floor.

Richard came running when she screamed.

"Why don't you ever put your tools away?" she cried.

"Let me see."

Reluctantly, she let him examine her foot.

"I think you need stitches."

"I just need a bandage," she insisted. "I'll be fine."

"No, that looks bad. You may need to go to the hospital."

After spending all day at the clinic, she hated the thought of another sterile environment but agreed to let him take her to the emergency room.

She used his sympathy as a cushion to deliver the news along the way.

"You know, how I've been sick to my stomach

84 | Janet Sierzant

lately?"

"Yeah, are you feeling better?"

"I'm fine, but... we're going to have a baby."

"What?" Richard looked stunned.

"I'm pregnant." She tried to read his face, but couldn't tell whether his expression was one of happiness or dismay.

"How many months?"

"I'm not sure. Maybe two." Dona hoped for early delivery or that he'd lose track.

*****

Dona looked at her son six months later, sleeping peacefully in her arms. Although it was too soon, she saw that his hair was much lighter than Richard's.

Sometimes, it's hidden in the genes, she told herself. Richard studied the boy's face. If he had any doubts, he kept them to himself.

Dona had renewed hope for her marriage. They planned a weekend barbecue for Steven's baptism. It was still warm, but the fall foliage provided a colorful backdrop.

Her mother and sister had arrived a few days earlier. Richard also invited his coworkers. One by one, Dona directed his friends to the backyard, where he was tending ribs on the grill. Last to arrive was Richard's secretary, Katrina.

"Where's Bill?" Dona asked.

Katrina shrugged. "We broke up." She looked a little sour.

Richard's gaze met hers, and he quickly darted away. Dona wondered why he hadn't mentioned it to her. Tensions hung in the air as Katrina popped open a beer.

Interrupting the uncomfortable conversation, Dona's mother approached them, Steven in her arms, with a trail of cooing guests following.

Later, Dona saw Katrina opening another beer. The woman acted drunk.

Curious, Dona walked over.

"Is something wrong?" she asked.

"It's Richard," Katrina slurred. "He's the reason Bill left me."

"Bill left because of Richard?"

As Katrina raised the beer to her lips, Dona noticed a small flower tattoo on her upper arm. She studied it intently. "Nice tattoo," she said. "What kind of flower is it?"

Katrina glanced at her shoulder. "It's a honeysuckle. That's my nickname."

Dona stared, recalling the email on Richard's laptop. *So, you're the bimbo missing my husband!*

"Richard lied. He said you were getting divorced. I wouldn't have screwed him if I'd known the truth."

Stunned, Dona rose from her chair and went back into the house. It could have been a turning point in her marriage. Instead, she tucked the information away in her bag of denials. It was easier to pretend it never happened and fall back into her comfort zone. Besides, she had had an affair too.

Dona liked to call Steven her 'Little Prince'. A

bright and cheerful child, his laughter filled the house and made her smile.

On the surface, they seemed like a perfect family. Richard said he would never hurt her, but it was hard to believe him.

Dona's sexual indifference soon became a problem and harder to hide. Her lack of response was all Richard's fault. Something inside her had changed after she found out he was having an affair. Maybe it was a mistake—a one-time lapse in judgment. As a rule, people don't change. She remembered Richard saying that his father once had an affair, but his mother forgave him. Perhaps it was ingrained in him from childhood.

She began making excuses—I'm tired, busy, or didn't feel well—anything to keep the distance between them. In the early years, she'd been the dutiful wife, enduring the act and feeling relief afterward because she wouldn't have to deal with it again for a few days. She no longer had the energy and motivation to work on their marriage.

Drowning in a sea of anxiety, Dona managed to stay afloat. Her buoyancy kept her from falling into a black hole of despair, but it also kept her paralyzed.

Dona wasn't happy with Richard. She didn't hate him, but hate would have made things easier. It was little things that made her want to leave him, like the sounds he made when he ate or the way he slurped his coffee. She wanted a divorce but didn't want to uproot the children, nor did she want to leave her house—all excuses.

# Chapter 18 | Cheater

### Richard

---

Through the years, Dona's two sons went in different directions. Richie was more like his father, loving the outdoors, but Steven was the studious type. Richard thought they'd spend hours together, camping, hiking, or hunting, but Steven preferred reading.

She loved being a homemaker. It was rewarding. The children kept her busy, and her homesickness for New York quelled. But as the years floated by, they demanded less of her time, and she grew restless. Now, she wanted to travel and experience new things.

Richie was the first to move out. He took a sales position in an international company and moved into his own apartment.

After graduating from high school with honors, Steven applied to the University of Colorado. Dona had hoped he would choose a school on the East Coast. Forced to leave his faithful dog behind when he took off for college, Steven asked Dona to keep him until he settled. Buck was a pound rescue that Dona adopted for Steven's tenth birthday. He followed her wherever she went. While the dog nosed around, tracking the scents of wild animals, she sipped her coffee and strolled around her garden. She savored the solitude. Old Buck was good company.

The house echoed with unfilled space after the children moved out. Sometimes it seemed quiet as a tomb. Her old fear of being abandoned had returned with a vengeance, a dull ache spreading through her chest. The house she had loved now filled her with apprehension as she paced the floor.

It was Dona's birthday, so Richard had mentioned going out to eat and then to a movie. Although she appreciated the sentiment, she declined to eat out but agreed to go to the movies. As they waited for a parking spot at the theater, a car beat them to it. Fuming, Richard cursed, glaring at the driver. Once in line for the ticket, Richard noticed the same man standing a few positions ahead of them.

"I'll be right back," he said, leaving her to pay for the tickets.

He returned with a devious smile.

"What did you do?" she asked.

After the movie, they exited the theater and walked to their car.

"My tires!" Someone yelled. "They're flat!"

"You're despicable!" Dona reminded herself—she never wanted to be on the wrong side of Richard.

Dona sensed her husband was still cheating. This time, Richard didn't try to hide it. Sometimes, he didn't even call her when he was late.

She wanted to confront Richard, but was too scared. She didn't do well with change. Richard seemed to do whatever he could to move her in that direction, but she didn't budge. Her life wasn't that bad. She could do whatever she wanted … if she didn't bring his secret lover into the light. He was still her husband. At first, she was terrified of losing him. It was easier to be complicit.

Frozen in time. That's how Dona felt. As much as she wanted her independence, she clung to the security of having someone in her life, even if he was a cheater.

By Christmas, Dona was at her lowest point. She was expected to be joyous, but couldn't get into the spirit. Instead, she counted the days until it was over. Some couples are soulmates, she thought. We're cellmates! She recalled Benjamin Franklin's words from history class. "Those who give up freedom for security deserve neither."

*What would it be like to live alone?* The thought consumed her. She made lists of the pros and cons of staying in the marriage, finding fewer and fewer cons as time passed. Dona broke into a cold sweat.

He often came home after she'd fallen asleep and was gone before she woke up.

Richard couldn't avoid her forever. She picked up the phone even though she knew he'd let it go to voicemail.

"Richard. I have something very important to discuss with you. Please come home."

Ten minutes later, he called her back. "What is it?"

"I'd rather not discuss it over the phone. Just come home for dinner tonight. It's important."

"I'll try to get out of work early, but I can't

promise."

Richard looked annoyed when he came through the front door.

"What did you want to tell me?" he demanded.

"Can we at least sit down to a civilized meal together?"

She gave him a plate of steak and potatoes, his favorite comfort meal.

He reluctantly sat down. They ate in silence.

"I want a divorce," she announced.

Richard looked stunned.

"I know all about your affairs."

"Oh, stop being so dramatic." His expression didn't change as he buttered another piece of bread and took a bite.

"We'll have to sell the house," he taunted.

It was a jab to her weak spot. He had a way of making her feel inadequate, and she suddenly felt unsure. Even though the house was unfinished, it was hard to let go of the dream. Part of her wanted to relent, but she held firm.

"I know."

"If that's what you want! That's what you'll get!"

Dona felt an anxiety attack coming on. She hadn't anticipated his immediate acceptance.

Richard pushed his chair back and put his dish in the sink. "I'll call my attorney and have him draw up the papers. You can keep the house, but the business is mine." He grabbed his coat and left.

Even though she was the one who initiated the divorce, she had a gut-wrenching feeling of abandonment. Alone in the kitchen, emptiness overwhelmed her, and she picked up the phone to call her mother.

"I'm sorry, sweetheart. I always suspected something was amiss between you, but I didn't want to interfere. What you need is a divorce lawyer."

"Richard is going to talk to his lawyer."

"I'd feel better if you found a good attorney of your own."

"Why?"

"You need someone who will look after your interests."

"Richard said I could have the house and even agreed to pay the mortgage for the townhouse we bought in Florida as a retirement home until it could be sold. We've been married for over twenty years. I don't think that Richard would want to hurt me."

Dona hired a lawyer anyway, but Richard honored his promise. As part of the divorce settlement, the split-level house awarded to her was in shambles. The roof leaked and needed repairs. Weeds grew through the cracks in the driveway, and the circuit breakers kept tripping. Dona feared other problems and always wondered what would go wrong next.

# Chapter 19 | Hawthorne Yellow

### *Dale*

---

Divorce was never something she had expected to face at this stage of her life. After all, the children were grown and out of the house. Things should have been easier. She felt mild regret that they couldn't get past their differences. Their marriage wasn't always horrible. There were moments of laughter and joy. They simply detached day by day until they became strangers.

It was sad to think she could end up alone in her old age. She'd never have the comfort of knowing they were there for each other if one of them should fall. She had to forget what Richard had done and who he had done *it with*. She'd never been one to live in the past. Dona threw herself headlong into her new life. She planned to sell the house in North Carolina and move to Florida. But before she could, the walls needed a fresh coat of paint and a long list of minor repairs.

Hawthorne Yellow! A home makeover show had promised it would brighten any space. But as she stepped off the ladder, paint dripping from the roller, she stood back and gasped. Dona hated it! A wave of depression reared its ugly head. "You never were a good decorator!" Richard's voice rattled in her brain, making her feel inadequate. She pushed the voices aside. *I'll just have to repaint! But not now! What I need is the Florida sun!* She left everything exactly as it was and packed her bags to head to her townhouse.

Once Dona was in Florida, she felt a heaviness lift from her. She listened to the ocean's breath as she walked along the shore, a gentle breeze kissing her cheek, as her feet crunched on pink sand speckled with tiny white shells. The rest of the world melted away as she soaked in the salty air. Lulled into the Florida lifestyle, she lost herself in paradise.

After two weeks of basking in the sun, she returned to tackle the problems in North Carolina. The brushes were stiff, and the paint cans were still on the tarp where she had left them. Now, she had to clean up the mess and was no closer to being finished. The paint swatch she had taken from the Florida townhouse was still in her purse — a unique textured paint. It was just what she needed to hide the cracks and dents in the walls.

Dona showed the sample to the clerk in the paint department at the home store, but he wasn't familiar with the product. Frustrated, she examined the paint card once more. On the back, it said the name of a specialty paint store. She found the paint and supply store only five miles from the house. Dona tucked the sample in her purse and drove to the store.

"Can I help you?" the clerk asked.

"I'm looking for textured paint. I've been to the home stores, and no one seems to know anything about this." She handed the sample to the clerk.

He smiled. "It's called '*Knock-Out*.' There's a contractor who comes in here for the stuff all the time. He specializes in this technique."

"Do you have his number?"

"Hey, Lou," he yelled into the back room. "Who's the guy who does wall texturing?"

Lou came out of the storage room. "We have his flyer around here somewhere." He searched under the counter. "Here it is! Dale. Dale O'Brien."

"Thank you so much." Back in her car, she dialed the number.

"Hi, is this Dale?"

"Yes, how can I help you?" he asked in a soft southern drawl.

"I'd like to get an estimate on texture painting for my house."

"Sorry. I'm really booked this week."

"Oh, please. I've been searching all over town. You're the only person who knows the technique."

"Well, I may be able to come tomorrow and take a look, but I won't be able to get to it for another week or two."

Dona gave him directions to the house. Her spirits lifted as she searched the internet for a real estate agent … one step closer to Florida.

# Chapter 20 | Southern Drawl

### *Dale*

The next day, when Dale arrived, Dona opened the door before he could knock. He jumped back. "You near about scared me to death, ma'am."

Dona stared into his translucent blue eyes. He smiled, dimples deepening on a square jaw that still hinted at his youthful good looks.

"I'm Dale."

"I'm sorry, I'm just so glad you're here."

"Are you Dona?"

"Yes. Please come in. I'll show you around."

Dale wiped his feet on the welcome mat and walked from room to room, examining the walls. She noticed he had a slight limp. "What happened to your leg?"

"It's an old hunting injury. Sometimes it acts up, especially when it's cold or humid."

"Oh, I'm sorry."

"You got a lot of cracks in your plaster."

"That's why I wanted it textured. I tried to do it myself, but I made a mess."

Dale nodded. "Sure enough, ma'am, you did."

"Can it be fixed?"

"All in good time," he said. "All in good time. This paint will cover the cracks nicely."

Dale seemed like a take-charge kind of guy. Scrutinizing the rest of the house, he put her on the spot. "You seem to have a lot of other things that need repairing, too."

"I know, but...."

"You should paint the ceilings, too."

"They haven't been painted in years," she admitted. "But...."

"The trim needs painting too, and some is missing."

Dona frowned. Richard had known a little about carpentry. He could build anything when he put his mind to it. But he could never finish a project, often stopping just short of the trim that would have tied it all together. Their house became a museum of unfinished projects.

"I can't afford to fix everything. I only want the walls painted."

"Well, as it turns out, I have eight cans of paint that a client ordered and canceled. I can give you a discount."

"What color is it?"

"Apple green."

"Nah. I was thinking more of a peach tone."

"All right, suit yourself."

Dona agreed to have him do minor repairs to sell the house quicker, but it would put a significant dent in her savings.

Before he left, Dale stopped in the kitchen. "Is that coffee I smell?"

"Yes, would you like some?"

"I sure would."

Dona filled a mug with fresh hot coffee. "How do you take it?"

"Light and sweet."

"Oh, dear. I'm afraid I don't have any sugar. I never touch the stuff."

"That's okay. I'll just take cream."

Dale drank the coffee, and then she walked him out to his truck. His bumper was covered with stickers. "Vegetables Ain't Food - They're What Food Eats," and "Ditch the Bitch, Let's Go, Hunting."

Dale looked like a redneck straight out of a Marshall Tucker Band concert. He noticed her reading them and grinned. "Are you from up North?"

"Yes, New York."

"I like a good city woman," he said, a smile spreading across his face. "Maybe we can go out on a date sometime."

Since her divorce, she hadn't considered dating.

Dale was one of those smooth-talking southern boys, and Dona was intrigued. *Maybe it'll be fun.*

"We'll see," she said, thinking that if she agreed, he might start working sooner.

For two weeks, Dale repaired and painted. Just as he promised, the interior of her house looked new and fresh. Now it was ready to be listed with the realtor. It was so nice that Dona was almost tempted to keep it. *Almost!* If she couldn't return to New York, Florida was where she wanted to be.

"Don't forget, you owe me a date," Dale said.

"I said I'd think about it."

"Come on now, you promised."

"Did I?" Dona didn't remember promising.

"Come on... They have Pioneer Days at the fairgrounds this weekend."

"I don't know..."

"You'll have a good time," he said. "I swear it!"

"Well, maybe..."

"Do you like country music? They have a dance floor and play country music."

Dona wasn't sure it was a good idea to get involved with someone soon after her divorce, but she felt so alone. *What's the harm in a little date?*

"All right, I'll go out with you, but I must warn you. I don't dance."

"All right, I'll see you then."

"What should I wear?"

"Jeans, of course! Do you have cowboy boots?"

"No, all I have are stiletto boots."

Dale laughed. "Those won't do. Just wear sneakers. You do have those, don't you?"

"Of course. I use them at the gym."

"Great! I'll pick you up in the morning. We'll make a day of it, and after that, we'll go for dinner. I know of a great little place for ribs where the meat falls off the bone. But don't worry. It's a casual place."

Dona brought two pairs of shoes—walking shoes for the streets and dress shoes to slip into heels when she arrived.

# Chapter 21 | Pioneer Days

*Dale*

---

On Saturday, Dale arrived at her front door with a bouquet of flowers.

"Let me put these in water." She breathed in their sweet fragrance. "Thank you."

He spat his chewing tobacco into the grass. Dona flinched, but reminded herself he was so good-looking. Surely, she could overlook the nasty habit—or at least try. Many men in the South enjoyed their chewing tobacco. Dona guessed he ate boiled peanuts, too. Still, she wanted to stay optimistic.

"I love that shirt you're wearing," she said.

"Thanks. My mother gave it to me. She has good taste in clothes." He followed her to the kitchen and watched as she arranged the flowers in a vase.

Like a true southern gentleman, Dale opened the passenger door of his truck and helped her up. Dona noticed the cane behind his seat but didn't think it was right to remark on it.

It was the first time Dona had the chance to attend Pioneer Days. The sights and sounds were unfamiliar to her. She felt as though she'd landed in some strange country and stepped back into a past era — booths lined up on either side of the pathway, displaying country placards and wreaths. Dale stopped at one stall with a sign that read "Daughters of the Confederacy." The woman behind the table smiled at him. "How's your Mama? Tell her not to forget. We have a meeting next Tuesday night, and we're counting on her being there."

"I'll be sure to tell her, but you know she wouldn't miss one of those meetings for nothing."

Dale's reverence for his mom was clear. She even influenced his professional decisions, his investment portfolio, where he lived, and who he voted for.

Comparing herself to his mother, Dona felt she came up short. Her thoughts were distracted by the smell of boiled peanuts.

Dale let out an audible sigh of pleasure. "I love boiled peanuts. Would you like some?" He dug through his pocket for the cash.

"No. But thank you."

"Suit yourself," he said and stuck his hand in the bag.

Dona tried not to cringe as he peeled the black shells and popped one after another in his mouth.

At least the weather was nice — warm but not hot, with a soft breeze. The music was loud, and it was impossible to carry on a conversation, but Dona smiled and nodded as Dale introduced her to his friends.

As the sun sank behind the trees, he said, "I made dinner reservations, so I reckon we should get going. I hope you're hungry."

"Famished." She stepped up her pace, and they were on their way.

The restaurant was a small country cottage with smoke billowing from the chimney. The aroma of slow-roasting pork filled the air.

Dale dashed over to her side, opened the door again, and offered his hand.

Inside, almost every table was occupied. The hostess smiled knowingly at Dale and led them to a table close to the dance floor.

"They know me here," he boasted.

"Especially the ladies, I see."

Dale grinned. "Ah, they don't hold a candle to you, darlin.' I think you're one of the most fascinating women I've ever met—that is, next to my mama."

Dona wanted to laugh, but sensed his sincerity.

Dale pulled out her chair and lifted the napkin off her plate. His excessive politeness was grating on her nerves.

"What can I get you, folks, to drink?" the waitress asked, handing them two menus.

"Bring us the best Irish beer on tap, darlin.' And we'll have two racks of them—their ribs." He looked at Dona. "You're gonna love 'em."

"What if I'm a vegetarian?" She joked.

Dale looked at her as if she were from a different planet. "Everyone loves a good pork rib." He didn't understand her New York sense of humor. Now that they were sitting across a table together, she realized they had nothing in common. They were complete opposites.

"Have you lived in the south all your life?" she asked.

"Yes, ma'am! Born and raised! I'm a real cracker. My great-daddy was a Confederate soldier."

Dona's eyes widened. "Did he fight for slavery?"

"Nooo!" Dale retorted. His voice was tinged with annoyance. "He fought for states' rights and the secession of the South! He fought for independence!"

"I'm sorry. We don't talk about the Civil War much up North." Her tongue tangled on the words. "I always thought that slavery was the main cause of the conflict."

"That's the problem with you, Yankees." His eyes darkened.

Dona was stunned by his quick temper. "Well, I'm American," she countered. "Down here, you're considered either a southerner or a northerner, and that's the problem with you rednecks."

"If the North is so great, maybe you should move back there."

"I guess we just have different ideas about it, "she said, trying to defuse the situation.

When the waitress came with his order, Dale picked up a rib and bit into it. They looked delicious, but Dona had lost her appetite. She poked at the meat on her plate and watched people two-step around the dance floor. Feeling uncomfortable, she was glad when the waitress came back to clear their plates.

"Would you folks like dessert?"

"I'll have a piece of your homemade pecan pie,"

Dale said. "How about you, Dona?"

"Just coffee, thank you."

"Cream and sugar?" the waitress asked.

"Cream. No sugar, please."

After his pie, Dale slid his chair back, making a scraping sound against the linoleum. He paid the check and drove her home. They made small talk as if the argument hadn't just happened. Dale tried to kiss her when he pulled in front of Dona's house, but she turned her head. "I have to get up early tomorrow," she said. "I have a busy day."

She stepped out of the truck without waiting for him to open the door. Dale shook his head and drove off.

Another angry man.

# Chapter 22 | Embedded

## *Thomas*

---

Dona wasn't happy about the split, but for the children's 6sake, she agreed to be civil. The divorce was amicable, and they remained on friendly terms. Their artful practice of compromise was a hallmark of their marriage. She let him keep the business, and he said she could keep the house. At the time, she thought it was generous, but soon realized the mortgage had to be paid, and without the business income she had always relied on, she didn't have enough.

"Why don't you rent out one of the boys' rooms for now?" Richard suggested.

"That's a great idea." Their two sons, Richie and Steven, were grown and out of the house.

Dona thought renting the downstairs apartment would be best.

Both studios had private entrances, but the upstairs apartment was Steven's right next to her bedroom. Only a hallway door separated the spaces.

She cleaned the room, stored the furniture and personal items in the garage, and then posted an ad.

By the end of the week, she had a potential renter. He had to duck his head to get out of his car.

"Hi, I'm Thomas Cleaver," he said and extended his hand. He was a tall man wearing a Stetson hat. For some reason, his size made her uneasy.

"Hi, I'm Dona. The apartment is kind of small," she said as she led him to the side entrance.

Thomas nodded as he looked around, but didn't seem impressed.

"I also have a studio apartment upstairs. It's bigger and has more windows." Instantly, she regretted mentioning it.

Thomas followed her to the outside stairs that led to the second-story room. "Oh, this will do nicely," he said.

"Actually, I was hoping to rent this room to a woman."

"My wife left me for another man and has custody of our three children. They're back in Texas, and I miss them terribly."

"Oh, I'm sorry to hear that," Dona said softly. He looked as if he was going to cry, and she felt a pang of sympathy.

"You won't regret renting it to me. I'm quiet. You'll hardly know I'm here. I work all week, and I go out of town every weekend. You can check my credentials." Thomas insisted. "I was just hired as a teacher at the high school."

The alarm bells in her head were oddly silent. She was eager to rent the room and, against her better judgment, ignored her instincts. *Maybe I'm reading too much into it.* Why would he urge her to check his background if he were questionable? A job at the school seemed to give him credibility. *Maybe it wouldn't be so bad having a man in the house.* Dona accepted his deposit and gave him the key. Still apprehensive, she asked Richard to install an extra lock. It took some getting used to having him in the house. Lying in bed, she could hear his every move in the next room. It kept her up most nights.

From the first day Thomas moved in, he annoyed her, constantly knocking on the door to borrow sugar, coffee, or something else. He always knew when she was home, even when she parked her car in the garage and tried to be quiet. She had no privacy. Sometimes, he waited for her to leave and rushed up before she could even get into her car. His obsession with her became all-consuming. He finally mustered the courage to ask her out, but she declined. He seemed offended at her rejection. She wished he would move out, but Thomas burrowed in like a tick.

Richard, a Vietnam veteran, had a short fuse. He suggested she serve Thomas with an eviction notice. It was that, or he would come over with his gun and instill fear in him. Waving a gun around was much too drastic, but it reassured her that Richard was there in case she needed him. Dona had always been afraid of firearms, partly because she didn't know how to shoot and worried she might use them if she lost her temper. It was rare, but she tended to bottle up her feelings until they burst out all at once.

One day, Dona and a family friend sat in the yard,

grilling hamburgers. Dona noticed Thomas on the side of the house. Before she could ask if he wanted to join them, he darted away.

Later, when she walked Scott to his car, Thomas came outside.

"Scott, this is my new tenant, Thomas."

Scott extended his hand, and Thomas shook it but didn't smile. She sensed his jealousy.

Thomas waited for Scott to leave, followed her into the house, and watched her through shifty eyes. She could smell the alcohol on his breath. Thomas liked his booze, and too much of it revealed a different side of him. She could tell he was over the line. His words slurred, and an unpleasant side of him surfaced.

"Is that your new boyfriend?" His nostrils flared with anger.

"I think it's time for you to leave," she said. "You're scaring me."

"I'm sorry," he said, changing his demeanor. "I didn't mean to upset you. Please forgive me."

"All right, but if you ever act this way again, I'll have to ask you to move out."

"I'll buy a gun and shoot myself."

"What?"

"I'm kidding, but you know I'd have no place to go."

His words scared her. *Would he really shoot himself? What if he decided to take me along for that eternal ride?"*

Dona watched Thomas from the living room window. His eyes were intense, a current of animosity just beneath the surface. He spotted her staring and smiled. It was strangely chilling. He had never shown any inclination toward violence, but she couldn't shake the feeling that Thomas was about to do something terrible. She was frightened. She told Richard about her concerns, and he agreed that Thomas had to go. Dona tacked a written notice to vacate within thirty days on his door, but hoped he would leave sooner. Renting wasn't worth the trouble. She needed to sell the house and move to Florida.

Thomas was home. As she drove up to her driveway, she noted a flicker of light through his window. She wondered if he had read the notice. After entering the garage, Dona turned off the car and sat for a moment in the dark. The automatic light turned on as she reached the front door, triggered by her movement. She cringed, every sound amplified in the silence. Once inside, she locked the deadbolt and stood very still so he wouldn't hear her.

All was quiet except for the faint sound of Thomas's television. She turned on the light and went into the kitchen for a glass of water. Tiptoeing upstairs to her room, she placed the glass on the shelf above her headboard.

As she was about to prepare for bed, the pictures on her wall began to bounce. Thomas was slamming things around. Like a man possessed, he yelled. "I'm not going anywhere."

A shiver ran through her. Terrified that he might break into her part of the house and attack her, she called the police. A car arrived in the area within minutes, its lights flashing. The two uniformed police officers approached Thomas to talk. Dona met them outside and explained what was happening. They seemed to be up there a long time. She couldn't breathe until they came down.

"Aren't you going to arrest him?"

"Ma'am, we talked to him, and he promised to calm down."

"But I want him to leave."

"Sorry, ma'am, tenants have rights, you know. We must follow the law. If you feel strongly about it, you can go to the courthouse tomorrow and file eviction papers."

The house was silent except for the floors, which creaked as he moved from room to room. She grabbed a knife from the kitchen drawer and brought it upstairs. Afraid to undress, she turned off the light and climbed into bed fully clothed, clutching the knife in the dark. *I'll evict him tomorrow!*

# Chapter 23 | Eviction

## *Thomas*

---

Dona hastily showered and dressed in fresh clothes early in the morning, hoping to leave the house before Thomas woke up. The courthouse was downtown. Frustrated, she drove around, looking for an empty parking space. Finally, she spotted a couple walking toward their vehicle. She stopped and flicked on her turn signal. They took forever to pull out, and the car behind her blared its horn. Usually, she would've waited it out, but the horn made her nervous. She reluctantly drove on and searched for another spot. Once parked, she entered the building and stood in line to go through security. The wire in her bra set off the metal detector, and the sharp beep startled her. She had to stand with her arms outstretched so they could pat her down.

"Where is the county clerk's office?" she asked the guard as he passed a wand over her body.

"Fifth floor," he said.

Dona stepped off the elevator and hurried to the window.

"I need to evict my tenant," she told the woman

behind the glass partition.

"Fill out this form, and don't leave anything out. You can sit over there," she said, pointing to a row of chairs in the waiting area.

When Dona finished the paperwork, five people were waiting in line. Time dragged on.

Finally, it was her turn. While the clerk typed out the information on the form, Dona explained her dilemma.

"I rented a room for this man, and he scares me."

The woman stopped typing and looked up. "Has he threatened you?"

"No, but I live alone, and lately, he's hostile. I want him out."

"We can serve him, but we can't do anything until he responds. Do you have another place to stay? Perhaps a friend or a relative?"

"Why should I leave my own house?"

"I just thought … Well, we'll notify you once the eviction notice is served. Until then, be careful."

Discouraged, Dona left the courthouse. Afraid to be home when the police arrived, she went shopping for the day.

On the way home, Dona saw a police car pulling into her driveway. She parked her car on the side of the road and waited.

Ten minutes later, the patrol car drove toward her. She stepped into the street and flagged it down.

The officer opened his window. "Can I help you, ma'am?"

"I noticed you were at my house. I filed an eviction

notice against my tenant. Is that why you were there?"

"No," he said with a puzzled look.

"You didn't serve papers of eviction?"

"No," he repeated.

She glanced in the backseat of the patrol car. There was Thomas in handcuffs, smiling at her—a sly, mocking smile. Her mouth dropped open in surprise. He seemed to be enjoying her distress. If the officer was still talking, she didn't hear him. All she could see was Thomas's taunting face. He rolled up his window and drove off.

Back home, she used the spare key to enter Thomas's apartment. His television was in pieces on the floor where he had hurled it the night before. There was also a large hole in the wall from his fist.

A letter was on the counter. It said, "You're going to pay for this. I hate you!"

Trembling, she called the courthouse. "I need information on an eviction I filed."

"Do you have a case number?" the clerk asked.

Dona read off the case number.

"Please hold."

It seemed to take forever. When the clerk finally returned to the line, Dona realized she'd been holding her breath.

"The eviction was not executed," she said. "There was a warrant out for this man. It was discovered last night when a police report was being entered. His real name is Timothy Clemons."

Her breath caught in her chest again. "What was his crime?"

"I can't give you that information, ma'am. All I can tell you is that he's now in custody. He goes before the judge in the morning, at which time he may be released on bail."

"Bail? What are the chances he'll make bail?"

"It depends on whether he's a flight risk. They could set it high or not at all."

"Does that mean he'll be coming back here?"

"Yes, if that's his registered address."

"No... I don't want Thomas—eh, Timothy, to come back. I'm scared to be here alone with him in my house."

"Is there someone you could stay with for now?"

"This is my house!

*****

The house was quiet that night, with Thomas in custody. Dona was exhausted but only dozed in an uneasy sleep.

The following day, at six, she gave up any attempts to sleep and went downstairs to make coffee. She sat on the bottom step of the hall, her emotions raw and exposed. She didn't want to leave, but a packed suitcase sat by the front door in case the judge released Thomas on bail. With the cordless phone in her hand, she wandered from room to room, keeping an eye on the clock above the kitchen sink. He was scheduled to appear before the judge at eleven, but she didn't know how long the hearing would take.

At noon, Dona called to find out the decision. A

busy signal drilled in her ear. As the pressure mounted, she couldn't wait any longer and drove to the courthouse. Her bra set off the alarm again. This time, she wasn't amused. Impatiently, she waited for the guard to run a scanner over her body. She pressed the elevator button for the fifth floor. It was taking forever, so she decided to take the stairs two at a time.

"I need information about an arrest."

"You're in the wrong place," the woman said. "This office is for evictions. You need to go up to the third floor."

Dona jumped onto the elevator again.

Breathless, she rushed up to the clerk. "I need information on a Thomas... I mean Timothy Clemons."

"Calm down and breathe," the young woman instructed. She clicked her mouse, and the computer screen lit up.

"They extradited him to Texas an hour ago."

"He's gone?"

"Yes. If you need to contact Mr. Clemons, you'll have to go through his lawyer."

"No, I'm fine," Dona said.

The following day, the police confiscated Thomas's car from her driveway. They found an array of questionable items in his trunk—plastic ties, handcuffs, and a roll of tape. He had a history of stalking women. He'd been a teacher in his hometown, feeding his obsession with access to female students. When he became obsessed with a young girl in his classroom, he abducted her, but she managed to escape. She'd been harboring a dangerous criminal. Dona hoped he would get the maximum sentence. *No more tenants!*

*****

By spring, the real estate agent had a potential buyer. Dona was relieved. The mortgage was already three months in arrears, and she didn't want it to go into default.

Arriving at the closing a half-hour early, Mr. Morrissey went through some last-minute paperwork. The real estate office had been there for a long time. Every piece of furniture was carved from wood, and the chairs were upholstered in leather. The scent of money was in the air. They sat at a long wooden table with thick varnish. There was a pitcher of iced water on a tray, accompanied by six glasses. Dona glided her hand across the glossy, cool surface to calm her anxiety.

John and Stephanie, the buyers, entered with their agent. Stephanie, a twenty-four-year-old girl with long blonde hair, pulled it back into a girlish ponytail. Her fresh face glowed with minimal makeup. Her husband, John, wore a suit jacket two sizes too big. It was apparent that they were in love, just at the beginning of their journey. Full of hope.

Their agent dragged another chair to the table across from Dona and Mr. Morrissey and unpacked a fat file.

"My clients have a few items that require attention

before we sign the papers. Most of their concerns are about unfinished projects around the house."

Dona felt herself shrink, even though it wasn't her fault. Richard never finished anything he promised. After a while, she stopped asking. She didn't want to be a nag.

Dona agreed to address their concerns. She felt lucky to have sold the house during a recession, even if she didn't get full value.

After paying the mortgage, she put the remaining money in the bank.

She walked away with less money but with the freedom to start a new life in Florida.

Now that she had a little cash, she worried less about the immediate future.

Then her phone rang. It was her lawyer.

"I have something to tell you, Mrs. Pearson—I thought you should know."

"What is it?"

"Richard has canceled your credit cards."

"I see." Her brow knotted.

Dona hung up. She had expected that might happen, but she thought Richard was being petty. Luckily, she had applied for her own credit card when their finances were sound.

# Chapter 24 | Man-hater

### The Green Room

---

Every time Joe dropped a new book through the door slot in the green room, Dona threw it in the corner. He promised! No romance books. She was about to throw the latest aside when she noticed the title, *The Hobbit*. It had always been her favorite—a world she could disappear into. Dona's only contact with the outside world was Joe, her captor. His questioning was her only source of entertainment. Dona craved human connection so much that she began to look forward to his visits on the computer—even though she knew it was crazy. She thought of Patty Hearst, abducted and brainwashed to become sympathetic to her captors. It was a known survival method, although Dona hadn't believed it at the time.

Now, she went along with Joe's endless questions, letting him pull her into long conversations. So long as he remained at a safe distance, she could tolerate his inquisitions.

When he appeared on the screen, Dona didn't wait for him to speak.

"You promised to let me go if I answered your

questions."

He laughed. "I'll never let you go."

"You're just like every man I know — making promises you never keep."

"So, you're a man-hater?"

"No… But men promise women the moon and the stars when all they want is money, sex, and someone to wash their underwear."

"Why so cynical?"

"I don't believe in fairy tales."

"Do men have any value to you at all?"

"Of course, but it's hard to find a man without an agenda. Most of them are sweet with a tinge of ulterior motive. I have a hard time with trust."

"Trust? Sometimes you must take a leap of faith. Maybe that can be tomorrow's subject."

*****

The tray slid into the room. It was the old familiar peanut butter sandwich. Joe was starting to get lazy. If I ever get out of this place, I'll never eat peanut butter again. At least there was milk and a cup of cold coffee to wash it down. She missed salmon and juicy, thick steaks. Even little things like soup — something she had taken for granted when she was outside. Most of all, Dona craved wine. She could easily become an alcoholic like her father if Joe provided it. Then she could block out reality and go limp like a rag doll.

Dona nibbled the sandwich, taking sips of milk in between. Climbing into bed with her coffee, she picked up the book. When she was married, she used to read herself to sleep. Now she had something to occupy her time. Soon, his words blurred into the pages. *Man-hater!* Dona's throat closed around the accusation, and it echoed through her mind.

Dona thought about Joe's questions. She hadn't always been a man-hater. As a young girl, she believed in fairy tales. Years of disappointment made her see it as foolishness—a folly that Disney drummed into a young girl's mind. Shortly after her divorce, she met John, who taught her that lesson. His love was the love she loved the most. Now she could hardly remember his face. She thought it was funny how old lovers faded.

Pacing the floor, Dona counted the steps across the length of the room and waited for Joe's morning intrusion. She had no idea how much time had passed since her abduction, but she'd been captive long enough for her thoughts to keep spinning to the past. "Panic attacks can be controlled," Dr. Fodor said. In her lucid moments, she knew her worries were irrational. Realizing that her heart rate was accelerating, she tried to take deep breaths like her therapist had instructed, but it wasn't working. Her son Steven always told her to think about something pleasant whenever she was about to hyperventilate.

She closed her eyes and tried to associate the color green with good memories. Burying her head in the pillow, she let the feeling take over, welcoming her to a peaceful slumber.

There was nothing else to do but sleep. It was her only escape. "Wake up," Joe's voice intruded on her dream. She heard him on the other side of the door telling her she could leave – or did he say she couldn't?

When she woke, Dona felt worse than before. She looked at the time. It was ten AM. Joe's image appeared on the screen. Dona studied the front of his desk. Old and weathered, it reminded her of the furniture in antique stores upstate. "Where are we?"

"I'm going out for a while. Is there something in particular you would like me to pick up?"

Dona tried to think. A map or a radio! Maybe then I can figure out where I am. *Fat chance* he'd fall for that!

"A television," she said. "I'm bored."

Joe laughed, amused by her request. "There's no reception out here. Besides, you're not missing anything. TV is all garbage. Information designed to keep the public stupid."

"Not all of it. There are documentaries and nature programs. My ex-husband used to watch them all the time."

"Smart guy!" He chuckled. "Did you love him?"

"He was a decent husband. When he wasn't cheating on me, that is."

"That's not what I asked. Tell you what, I'll get you something to read. What do you like? Romance? Mystery? Suspense?"

"Anything but romance."

"You sound bitter. Haven't you ever been in love?"

"Actually, yes, but it didn't turn out too good – he

was a sociopath."

"Ahh. You're quick to label people."

"If it quacks like a duck, it's a duck."

"Maybe you misjudged him."

"Perhaps... but it doesn't matter now."

He laughed. "Probably the wrong man. Okay—no romance books. Maybe I'll throw in a deck of cards. You can play solitaire."

# Chapter 25 | Rockefeller

## John

---

After the divorce, Dona lamented the wasted years, feeling like a failure at love. Refusing to look back, she threw herself into her new single life.

Her girlfriend had suggested she join a dating site. She chose one based in New York City. After her date with Dale, she decided she couldn't relate to the Southern mindset. Right away, men wanted to connect with her. She examined their profile photos and wondered if they were recent.

Dona hadn't meant to fall for John, but it happened fast—heat, charm, the kind of attention that fills every empty space. He messaged her daily. Although he wasn't handsome, there was something about him—a magnetism she couldn't deny.

Over the next two months, they exchanged phone calls and flirtatious text messages. John wanted her to come to New York to meet in person, but Dona wasn't sure she was ready.

"No stress, no pressure," he assured her.

She booked a room at the Hilton on 6th Avenue. They decided to meet at a restaurant near Rockefeller

Center, an Art Deco section of midtown Manhattan known for its grand plaza and ice-skating rink. She was surprised when John told her he had made reservations at The Rainbow Room. The restaurant was located on the roof, offering sweeping panoramic views of the city. Reservations had to be made well in advance. *Wow, he must have connections.*

*****

At Rockefeller Center, she rode the glass elevator to the sixty-fifth floor. She could see the Chrysler Building from the observation deck as it peeked through the low-hanging clouds. She was on the Top of the Rock.

"Welcome to the Rainbow Room," the hostess said. "Do you have a reservation?"

She clicked some keys on her computer. "Yes, I have it right here. John hasn't arrived yet, but you can wait at the bar."

Dona reveled in the breathtaking view. She'd once gone to the Statue of Liberty on a field trip in elementary school, but beyond that, she took New York for granted. She had lived in the city for most of her life but had never had the opportunity to truly enjoy what it had to offer.

Waiting for John, she sat at the bar and looked at the skyline. He was late, and she worried he might have stood her up. About to leave, she spotted him across the room. Dona recognized him from his photos. Wearing casual black pants with a gray button-down shirt, he walked in with a swagger as if he owned the place. Her heart raced like a colt at the gate.

After a few words, the maître-d' disappeared into the cloakroom and returned with a jacket. John put it on and approached the bar, never losing his smile.

"Sorry, I'm late. I was held up with an important business meeting."

"That's all right. I've been enjoying the view."

"It's so nice to be face-to-face finally," he said with a twinkle in his eyes. "You're exactly how I imagined you."

The hostess came up to them. "Your table is ready, sir." She showed them to a table by the window.

"Will this table be suitable?"

"Excellent," John said and handed her a fifty-dollar bill.

He ordered a scotch on the rocks and leaned back in his chair. He peered deep into her eyes as if he could see her naked soul.

Dona blushed under his intense gaze. "What part of New York are you from?"

"Upstate—just down the road from Bethel Woods. You know, the site of the Woodstock festival."

"That's exciting. How did you end up there?"

"My ex-wife has family there. She's Jewish. Like other Jewish New Yorkers, they go there for summer vacation. The whole community. They put up high fences for privacy, so people passing by can't see the cluster of cabins they occupy. Anyway," he continued, "we bought some horses and needed a place to keep them, so we bought an old barn."

"I just came back from California, but I don't care

for the West Coast."

Dona smiled. "I'm an East Coast girl. I'm happy living in Florida, but I miss New York."

"You're not really a New Yorker!"

"What?"

"You've been away too long. You lost your rights."

Dona laughed. "What about you?"

"I was working on a job there, but it's finished now. I never intend to leave New York, even though many women probably wish I would."

It was refreshing to be with someone so happy. John had her laughing so hard she almost choked on a piece of lobster tail. He had that cynical humor only New Yorkers would understand. Every time he smiled, his eyes sparkled. She was smitten.

As the sky darkened, a full moon rose.

"Do you have children?" John asked.

"Yes, two boys, Richie and Steven. One's in college and the other travels for his job. What about you?"

"I have two children also, a girl and a boy, but I haven't spoken to them in five years."

"Really? Why?"

"My ex-wife. She turned them against me."

"That's terrible. What happened?"

"She was having an affair with the landscape guy. When I found out, we had a big fight. She kicked me out and moved her lover into the house. Now they call him Daddy."

"Oh, I'm so sorry. You must miss them."

"On top of that, the bitch froze our bank account. I was left with nothing except the barn. I kicked the horse out and made it my home."

"You live in a barn?"

"Yeah. It's not so bad."

Dona found his story incredible. If he was manipulating her to feel sorry for him, it worked. He seemed so vulnerable — yet another thing they had in common. She wanted to protect him and take away his pain.

The restaurant slowly cleared out. Dona hadn't thought about how the evening would end.

John raised his arm with a theatrical wave to get their waiter's attention. He hurried across the restaurant, probably hoping for another fifty after hearing he was a big tipper.

"Check, please."

The waiter scrambled off and came with the check.

"I'll take your credit card, sir."

John pulled out his wallet and counted out $250. He threw it on the table and pulled his chair away.

"Cash is king," he said with a sly smile.

As they left the restaurant, he turned to her. "Why don't we check out the Christmas tree? They turned the lights on last week."

Arm in arm, they strolled down Fifty-Eighth Street. Dona floated down the street, light as air.

As they stood under the massive tree, his hand brushed against hers, sending shivers up her spine.

"Are you cold?" he asked, putting his arm around her shoulder.

Dona looked into his eyes and felt a rush in her heart. When he kissed her, it took her breath away.

"Why don't we go back to your hotel?" he said with a wicked grin.

"I don't know." It was almost midnight, and Dona was tired, but she didn't want the evening to end.

"We're both single," he coached, "and you can't deny the attraction between us."

Seduced by his glib charm, she found him to be more interesting than any other man she had known. The wine had lowered her inhibitions. She felt entitled to a one-night stand.

At the hotel, they giggled as they took the elevator up to her room. Out of the public eye, they fell back onto the bed. She succumbed to the passion that had built up all evening. John wrapped his arms around her in a hug, but it felt more like a restraint than affection. That night, she woke to find his arms locked around her body, pinning her in place. She couldn't move.

"John," she whispered.

He didn't answer. His grip tightened.

Something inside her twisted, but she lay still and stared out the window at the glittering lights of the New York skyline.

# Chapter 26 | Only the Lonely

## *John*

---

By morning, he was all sunshine. Boyish and affectionate, as if nothing had happened.

"What time is your flight?" he asked, his eyes closed.

"It's not until one o'clock, but I have to leave early to catch the bus to the airport."

"Then I guess we should get dressed. Do we have time to grab a cup of coffee?"

"I think so." She tried to shake off her disappointment. She had hoped they would make love again, but figured he wasn't in the mood.

Although the hotel had a restaurant, he preferred to go to the deli down the street. With coffee to go, they sat outside on a bench.

"Are you on Facebook?" she asked.

"Yes, but I go by a different name."

"Why?"

"It's complicated." He laughed.

"What is?"

"I'm just a very private person. I don't like people knowing my business."

"Then why are you on Facebook at all?"

"I like to keep tabs on my kids."

His explanation seemed suspicious, but she had no reason to doubt him.

"So, what are your plans when you get home?" he asked.

"I'll pack up and head to Florida for the winter."

John's eyes widened. "Do you have a place there?"

"Yes. My ex-husband kept the business. I got the house in North Carolina, and he agreed to pay for the townhouse in Florida until I could take over the mortgage."

After their coffee, John walked her to the Grand Central Terminal and kissed her goodbye. Thinking she'd never see him again, she put him out of her mind. After loading her suitcase, she boarded the bus. Her phone chimed with a text from John.

"Maybe I'll come and visit you in Florida!"

*****

Dreams about her townhouse in Florida swirled in her head. She imagined the large iron gates swinging open like welcoming arms to admit her into her new community. She pulled into the driveway, pressed the remote on the visor, and the automatic door to her garage opened. Once inside, she waited for it to close before getting out of the car. Tired, Dona left her suitcase in the car and entered the house. The humidifier was running quietly. The smell of emptiness filled the air. She ascended the stairs to her bedroom and crawled between the sheets.

She awoke to the sun streaming through her window and slipped into her swimsuit. Then she poured herself a cup of coffee and grabbed a towel to sit by the pool. It became a morning ritual. Dizzy with love, she chatted with John on the phone for hours. Dona felt they were soulmates, and destiny had brought them together. Their romance was getting serious, but he was 1,200 miles away in New York. All they could do was text and call. Her breath hitched every time the phone chimed, and her heart skipped a beat.

"We are golden," John said. "Our love is perfect."

Dona gobbled up his words like a hungry baby bird. When he called to say he was on his way to Florida, she was as giddy as a schoolgirl.

Anticipating his arrival, she cleaned and shopped for food—steaks, lobsters—she spared no expense. Dona wanted to show off her cooking and baking skills.

Music streamed through the stereo—*I Only Have Eyes for You* by the Flamingos. She'd listened to it countless times while daydreaming about him.

Finally, she heard John's car pull into the driveway and rushed to open the door. His smile was just as she remembered.

John scooped her up in his arms. "Did you miss me?"

She answered him with a long, passionate kiss. "I'm so happy you decided to come to Florida. Come on in."

"Wow, this is a nice place!"

"Thanks."

"I smell cookies," he said.

"Yep, I've been baking all day to keep busy."

Like an eager child, he spotted the dish of cookies on the kitchen counter and popped one in his mouth. "That's so good." He reached for two more.

"I made dinner."

"This is dinner," he said.

Dona laughed.

After a dinner of steak and potatoes, they sat outside and gazed at the night sky. Twinkling stars framed the pale crescent moon. John pointed out the constellations Orion, Pegasus, and the Big Dipper.

"Look. Isn't that the North Star?"

"Yes, we should make a wish," he said and yawned.

"You must be exhausted from driving all day," she said.

"Not too tired." He pulled her to him, kissing her until she was dizzy, and then nibbled on her earlobe. "Let's go to bed." He led her up the stairs to her bedroom.

After shedding their clothes, Dona slipped under the covers.

"Don't be shy," John said, pulling them away.

As they made love, Dona closed her eyes and let him take her to places she'd never been. It felt more intense than their first time. Soaring through the clouds, she landed softly against John's chest. His rib cage rose and fell beneath her.

Content, she sighed. Soon she was fast asleep.

Dona didn't want his visit to end. They walked along the beach for the next four days, watching the evening sunsets after a home-cooked meal. The rest of the time, they spent in bed.

On the last night, John declared his love. Dona could hardly believe her ears. She forgot about the lonely, divorced woman she had been six weeks before.

"I don't want you to leave tomorrow," she whined.

"Maybe I should move to Florida."

"I thought you were moving to California."

"Now that I've met you, I may have to rethink that. Or, maybe you can move to New York once you sell your house."

"No, thank you. It took me a long time to get to Florida. I love the warm climate."

"Why Florida? Why can't we live someplace like the Bahamas or Aruba?"

"Aruba?" Dona asked, smiling at his recklessness.

"Why not? We're free to live wherever we want. Just think. We'd lie on the beach all day drinking margaritas and make wild, passionate love to each other every night."

"That sounds like a dream."

"It's in our power to make our dreams a reality."

Everything about him fascinated her, yet there was so much more to learn.

"Take a leap of faith," he told her.

To Dona, faith wasn't rational. If it were, she'd have an easier time leaping. John insisted that they live together. Things were changing so fast. She barely had time to absorb it all.

As much as she was drowning in love, it took her so long to gain her independence, and she wasn't sure she wanted to live with someone again so soon.

# Chapter 27 | Bullseye

## *Richard*

---

One morning, she went out to her car in the driveway and noticed a gash in one of the tires. Someone stuck a blade into the sidewall. Dona rummaged through the glove compartment for her AAA card, only to discover it had expired. Then she remembered a spare in the trunk. *How hard could it be?*

The sun was directly above her as she positioned the jack under the axle. It was more complicated than it looked, and soon sweat poured into her eyes. Dona managed to get the car high enough to remove the lug nuts, but the wheel simply spun. She had to lower the car again until the wheel sat on the ground to remove them. The last one wouldn't budge. The handle was too short, and she couldn't get enough leverage. She collapsed on the ground and buried her face in her hands. *What now?* She went back into the house to think about it. *If I had leverage, maybe I could...* She went to the garage and grabbed a three-foot pipe to extend the lug nut tool handle. *Voilà!* The lug nut came loose. She raised the car again.

While she was changing the tire, she noticed a

black car driving past the townhouse. For a second, she thought it was Richard. *No, it couldn't be. That was probably my imagination,* she thought. *Richard drives a white truck.*

The following day, the coffee maker gurgled and belched in the kitchen, and the scent of fresh coffee drifted up the stairs. Dona opened her eyes and thought about John. Like a drug surging through her veins, she couldn't get enough of his sexy voice. She couldn't believe how lucky she was to have met him.

She was about to go to the pool with her coffee and cell phone when she spotted a figure lurking on her front lawn. Dona opened the door and was shocked to see Richard standing there. He looked older. His hair was grayer, and his clothes were wrinkled and disheveled. He tended to turn up unannounced and enjoyed the element of surprise.

"Richard, what are you doing here?"

"I hoped we could talk."

Since their divorce, he'd had several girlfriends and always claimed he was over her. Whatever he did and whomever he did it with was no longer her concern.

"You could have called."

"I heard you're dating some handyman."

"John's not a handyman. He's a contractor. He has his own business."

Richard rolled his eyes. "Whatever! Is it serious?"

"Why do you care?"

"Well, I was hoping we could salvage our marriage."

"Richard, we've been apart for almost a year. I've moved on."

"Maybe we could try for a few months."

"We tried for years. I wasn't happy. What makes you think things can change in months?"

"All I want is for you to consider it. Think of our boys. They would be so happy if we got back together."

"I'm sorry, Richard. It's too late."

"Why are you always so negative?"

"I'm not negative. I'm realistic." Dona swore she wouldn't defend herself from his criticisms anymore, but Richard knew her soft spot.

"I don't have to talk to you," she hissed. "We're divorced."

"We didn't have to be. You never gave it a chance."

Dona was tempted to bring up the affair with honeysuckle, but held her tongue. Besides, it no longer mattered.

"We weren't happy," she said.

Richard shifted his weight onto one leg and crossed his arms across his chest. "You're never happy," he sniped. "Even the kids thought you were nuts. That's why Steven left the state. I lost my son because of you."

"No, he left to get away from you." Dona tried to quell the fury inside her, but rage tickled the back of her throat.

"He's not your son!" she snapped, but it was too late. The words hit were already out of her mouth — they hit Richard like an arrow to the heart.

Dona saw the coldness in his eyes as he turned his back to her and walked away.

"Good luck with your boyfriend," he muttered. "He's nothing but a swindler."

Dona slammed the door and leaned back against it with her eyes closed.

She hadn't meant to tell him about Steven. Her heart fluttered like birds flying off before a storm. *Maybe he didn't believe me,* she thought. *If he did, there would be hell to pay!*

Richard could be vindictive when he was angry. She wondered what he might do to hurt her.

# Chapter 28 | The Pendulum Swings

## *Richard*

---

The phone rang as Dona opened the front door. She picked it up just in time. "Hello," she said. No response. About to hang up, she heard an automated voice.

"We are calling to inform you that your mortgage payment has not been received."

Dona pressed zero for an operator.

"How can I help you?" a representative asked.

"I need help with my mortgage."

"I'll need your loan number."

Dona gave her the number and anxiously waited. *I knew it! Richard's trying to get even with me.*

"This loan is in default," the agent said. "Are you calling to make a payment today?"

"No, my husband and I are divorced. The court ordered him to make the payment."

"I'll have to transfer you to another department. Please hold."

Another automated message filtered through. "This is an attempt to collect a debt. Any information obtained will be used for that purpose."

*Debt*. Dona hated the sound of it. She bit her lower lip.

Richard is trying to force me out, she thought.

Once the agent came on the line, she repeated her personal information. She explained that her ex-husband was supposed to make the loan payments.

"Is your name listed on the loan?"

"Yes."

"Then you are also responsible. If you're having trouble making your payments, we offer a modification program that may help. Still, I will need your husband's consent."

Feeling defeated, she hung up and watched the blood-red sun sink below the treetops from her living room window. It hung over the treetops and slowly disappeared from view. Even though her problems were mounting, there had to be a silver lining. After a long walk around the neighborhood, she returned to the empty house. A surge of loneliness swept over her. Exhausted, she climbed the stairs to bed. As soon as she fell asleep, the phone woke her.

"What are you doing?" John asked.

"It's two a.m. I'm sleeping, silly."

"You're not going to hang up on me, are you?"

"Not a chance," she giggled.

"Good. I have this intense feeling about us. I want you to visit me."

"It's January, much too cold for me. Besides, I don't have winter clothes."

"I'll be your winter clothes."

Dona laughed. "Maybe I'll come in the spring."

"I'm counting on it," he said. "Now, go back to sleep and dream about me."

Dona hugged her pillow, pretending it was him, and fell back asleep.

*****

The following day, her son, Steven, called to check up on her. Feeling anxious, she wondered if Richard had said something about not being his biological father.

"How are you doing at school?" she asked, hoping to steer the conversation.

"Great. I love it here. Have you heard from Dad lately? He said he was working on a surprise. I think it had to do with you."

"He showed up here a week ago. He wanted to get back together, but I told him no."

"Oh, that must have hit him hard."

"I guess so because he stopped paying the mortgage on the townhouse. It may go into foreclosure."

"You may not have a choice."

"I'm happy in Florida! I don't want to leave!"

"Try to sell it before the bank forecloses. You can buy another townhouse or maybe rent an apartment."

"I'll think about it."

"Okay, Mom. Let me know if there's anything I can do to help. Maybe I can talk to Dad."

"No! I mean, thanks, honey, but I don't want to drag you into this. Maybe I'll find a realtor and ask about a short sale."

"That sounds like an excellent idea. At least you'll save your credit."

Dona never pictured herself in an apartment. She didn't have enough money to buy another townhouse, but she was determined to stay in Florida. She googled the nearest real estate office and gathered her mortgage paperwork. On the way, she stopped to see if any manatees were swimming in the canal. Then she stopped at the post office to pick up her mail. The temptation to do a little shopping was great, but she couldn't procrastinate any longer.

He seemed to back off when she told John she was losing her house.

"I guess I won't be moving to Florida," he said.

"Then we won't be together."

"Maybe you could move here."

"Maybe."

Florida was supposed to be her fresh start. She wasn't ready to give that up—not yet. Tired, she slipped into bed and closed her eyes, but couldn't sleep. The tick-tock of the Westminster chime clock her father had given her echoed in rhythm with her thoughts.

# Chapter 29 | Free Love

## John

---

The agent found a buyer by spring, and Dona made arrangements to move to New York. Knowing someday she would return, she arranged to have all her belongings transferred to a storage unit. The Westminster clock was the last item to be packed. As it struck eleven, she waited for the melodic tune to finish before removing the pendulum and carefully wrapping it in a newspaper, along with the weights. As the movers carried out the last box, she took one more walk through the house. Her footsteps echoed on the bare wood floors.

Bethel called itself the town of love and rock and roll—a haven for dreamers and left-over hippies from the Woodstock Era. Surrounded by fertile, rolling farmland, it was a down-to-earth place. Many hippies had settled there after the Woodstock Festival, so the people were laid back. The best thing about Bethel was that Manhattan was only ninety minutes away by train. As she snaked along the quiet rural roads, she noticed the old frame houses that had weathered untamed winters. Most needed a fresh coat of paint.

Even the potholes warned of the upcoming salted roads when snow took over. Growing up, she recalled the holes filled with muddy water after the snow melted.

John's house wasn't really a house—it was a barn. The yard was meticulously manicured; its gentle landscape extended as far as the eye could see. Hedgerows protected the boundaries of his property.

Although the interior needed repairs, the walls displayed expensive art, including paintings of every genre. There was no consistency, but somehow, it worked.

After dinner, they sat outside on the porch. Under a dome of the endless night sky, she felt as if she had left the planet—removed from the daily stress of figuring out which direction her life should go.

"Look at all those stars," she said.

"Look at me." His eyes searched hers in the dim moonlight and came alive with wicked amusement. They held her captive as if they were trying to possess her. "Let's go get comfy."

"Comfy?" *What an odd word.*

He pulled her toward him and kissed her. "Let's go upstairs."

By the end of the evening, it didn't take much persuasion for him to talk her into bed. Everything about him fascinated her, yet there was so much more to learn. Locked together in heated passion, she melted into the moment and slipped into ecstasy.

The morning was blissful, with birds singing and a cool breeze drifting along the Mongaup River. The wide, open spaces and fresh air helped her to think more clearly. *Richard would love this place.*

John and Dona sat outside, drinking coffee. The sky was crystal blue, but there was a bite in the air. She wrapped herself in his so-called *man-blanket*. It had a southwestern pattern on one side and a fur lining.

"There's something different about the air in the North," she said. "It's thinner, crisper."

"I think it has to do with the altitude, Get dressed," he said. "I'd like to take you to where they held the Woodstock Festival."

"That sounds like fun."

Dona ran back into the house and pulled on her jeans and a sweater.

As they drove through winding country lanes, they passed farms with cows grazing in the high grasses between colorful patchworks of poppies and wildflowers. Some abandoned houses appeared to be on the verge of collapse. Dona thought it would be fun to explore, but John told her it was too risky because the roofs weren't very sturdy and sometimes collapsed under the weight of fallen snow.

John parked outside the Performing Arts Center but didn't buy admission tickets. Instead, they walked around the free exhibits and then lounged in the grassy field where thousands of people once camped and took mind-trips forty years ago. John told her about the events they had every summer.

"If you're a good girl," he teased. "I'll take you to a concert here. You wouldn't believe how many people attend. There's always a long line of cars parked against both curbs." He looked pensive. "This area is a goldmine."

"How so?"

"Tons of people come here from the city every weekend. There aren't any motels around, so they stay in Monticello. I was thinking about renting my place out."

"Where would you stay?"

"Oh, I don't know. It was just a thought."

John took a long way home and detoured to Kauneonga Lake. They passed under a canopy of spruce trees. The soft fragrance wafted into the car, and Dona breathed in deeply.

"Every winter, they build a large ice sculpture when the lake freezes over. I think it's a lion. People will ice skate around it until spring. The ice weakens until it can't support the lion, and the lion plunges under the water. It's a warning to the skaters that they're on thin ice! Thin ice, get it?" He laughed without amusement. "Then, next year, we do it all over again."

Dona settled into the town and began meeting locals. The postal worker always had a smile, and the liquor store owner went out of his way to point her to the best wines.

There was never a dull moment with John. Sometimes they went tubing down the river. The water was icy but refreshing. The peaceful lifestyle made her feel safe.

He paid cash for everything, which made Dona wonder. She used her American Express card all the time. It was so much easier.

"Don't you believe in credit cards?" she asked.

"Nah, I haven't had one in years. It's too easy to get in trouble with those things. Besides, they wouldn't give me credit if my life depended on it."

"Is your credit bad?"

"I don't want to talk about it."

John rarely complained about his past, but he worried about his future. He had champagne tastes on a beer budget and a closet full of financial skeletons. Any riches he claimed he had were given to him by other women.

John was beside her in the morning, his legs threaded through hers. She reached over and touched his chin, stubbly with tiny gray hairs. He moaned.

"What should we do today?" she asked.

"It's Friday. Let's go pickin'."

"What's that?"

"Garage-sale hopping—you wouldn't believe the stuff people sell. I once purchased an entire antique bedroom set, complete with a matching desk. It was real oak with intricate carvings. They don't make 'em like that anymore."

# Chapter 30 | Shyster

## *John*

---

The area was rich in history, and consignment stores were filled with hidden treasures and trinkets from estate sales. They spent the afternoon drifting from one garage sale to another. When there weren't any more, he suggested antique stores.

At the first antique store, John scanned the display cases.

"I love to sift through items for anything worth more than their appraisal. Then I sell them on eBay. It's an easy buck."

"It all looks like junk to me!" she teased.

He pointed to an old watch. "I once had one like this."

An elderly man unlocked the case so he could examine it.

Holding the jeweled watch up to the light, John said, "I have to have it."

"Didn't you say you have a Rolex?"

"Yes, but you can never have too many watches." He dug in his pocket, then froze.

"Dona, I left my wallet on the kitchen table. Lend

me one hundred dollars? I'll give it back when we get home."

Put on the spot, she didn't dare refuse.

When they returned home, he flopped down on the couch. "I'm beat."

Dona slid next to him. "Do you have my money?"

His expression changed from a smile to a scowl, and his eyes turned cold and steely. John jumped up to get his wallet.

"Here's your money!" he snapped and slapped five twenty-dollar bills on the counter.

By night's end, his charm had returned-- quick wit and all.

In the middle of the night, she woke to find his arms tightly around her. It felt as if she was in a straitjacket. Slipping from his grasp, she went downstairs.

Outside, the wind howled. The porch light was the only source of light, casting restless shadows across the walls. The hollow breath of winter sent a shiver down her spine. Pressing her head against the sliding glass doors, Dona peered outside, searching for wildlife. John claimed coyotes and bears were on his property. The only beast she saw was inside the house. Deep down, she sensed something wasn't right about him, yet she returned to his lair and crawled back beside him.

*****

That lusty evening they spent together in New York

haunted Dona. The illusion of love kept her hopeful.

After a fitful night's sleep, Dona opened her eyes and looked over at John lying beside her. Gentle puffs of air escaped his lips. His disheveled hair made him look like a little boy—so innocent—nothing like the volatile man she'd seen the night before. She went downstairs and put a pot of coffee on. Soon, he joined her.

"Good morning, Dona," he said in a cheery voice.

She didn't answer.

"Where'd you go last night?" he asked.

"I couldn't sleep."

"You can't leave without telling me."

Dona laughed. "Why not?"

"Because I'm the boss of you."

Dona looked up, about to retaliate, but saw his smile.

"What's wrong?"

"Nothing."

"So, you're not going to talk to me anymore?"

"I don't know what you want me to say."

His eyes sparkled with wicked delight. "You can't leave if that's what you're thinking. I'll lock you up and throw away the key."

Dona couldn't help laughing. He seemed completely different now.

"You know I love you," he said, turning on the charm.

She wanted to believe him, but he sent mixed signals.

They took their coffee outside. The leaves had begun to turn on the trees, gliding gracefully to the lawn. It was her favorite time of year, but the icy breath of winter would soon be upon them. It sent a shiver down her spine.

*****

The economy took a downturn, and John had no work. She clung to the hope he would find a job and revert to the man she had fallen in love with. At first, she was open to giving him the money he needed to get on his feet. She saw it as an investment in their future, but a noticeable crevice had opened between them.

That night, a Facebook message landed in her inbox. "He wants your money. Get out!

Dona felt crushed. She didn't want to believe it, but she knew enough about John that the warning couldn't be dismissed.

"Dona, I have to ask a big favor."

"What is it?"

"I need to pay the electric company, or they'll shut us down."

"Why?"

"My payment is two months late."

"I don't know."

"Either that or you can put the electric in your name. You don't want to take cold showers, do you?"

"No, but putting my name on your account might be risky."

"We're a couple," he said, "and couples help each

other. Don't you trust me?"

"Yeah, but…."

"Stop being so stingy." His eyes glazed over. "I have a side job next week. You'll get your money back."

When she first met John, she thought his recklessness was cute. But now she had doubts about his morality.

She recalled taking a ride with him to Staten Island. He breezed past the toll booth.

"Don't we have to pay?" she asked.

"Nah, I borrowed a toll pass from a car in the shop. I'll put it back tomorrow. They'll never know it was missing."

She recalled taking a ride with him to Staten Island. He breezed past the toll booth.

"Don't we have to pay?" she asked.

"Nah, I borrowed a toll pass from a car in the shop. I'll put it back tomorrow. They'll never know it was missing."

"You're a shyster," she said. John was nothing more than a petty criminal. He lived on the edge of the law and tried to drag her with him — Bonnie and Clyde. From a safe distance, his antics had amused her. But as her life became tangled with his, it became harder to detach. If this woman was telling the truth, it was only a matter of time before he tripped up.

# Chapter 31 | Taking Control

## John

---

Dona heard the food tray hit the floor. Like Pavlov's dog, she sprang up to retrieve it. An Egg McMuffin with cheese. She glanced at the night table. The clock read seven. *This must be breakfast.*

She peeled off the cheese and took a bite. It was cold, as if it came straight out of the refrigerator. Disgusted, she threw it aside and drank the coffee while waiting for her captor to make another appearance on the computer.

As if he read her mind, his voice came from the speaker.

"Good morning."

"No, it's not. What do you want to ask me now? Let's get on with it."

"You women are all alike—always trying to take control of a man's life and stingy as hell."

"Have you ever considered that maybe we aren't trying to control men, just trying to hold onto our own lives and security?"

"Is that why you play games?"

"It's all a game, and men seem to have the

advantage."

"Don't you think couples should help each other?"

"In what way? Financially?"

"Yeah, if they need it."

"Men should be self-sufficient. They shouldn't have to rely on a woman for money."

"Well, why would that be any different than a wife living off her husband?"

"Because women work just as hard at home. They care for the children, clean, shop, and cook."

"Yeah, and they get to stay home eating bonbons while the man has to go out and do manual labor."

"That's the problem with men today. They're jealous of their wives. They want to stay home too. I have no respect for an unmotivated man."

Joe's face was hidden behind his ski mask, but his eyes said he was fuming. He mumbled something incoherent, then abruptly shut off the camera.

Joe's sudden anger reminded Dona of the day John had worked himself into a seething rage because she didn't want to go along with his plan to build an extension on his house.

She was on her second cup of coffee. The aroma brought John downstairs.

Dona handed him a cup. "Sorry, I forgot to buy sugar."

"You wouldn't forget if you used it in your coffee," he said. Taking a sip, he made a sour face. "Sit down. I have a business proposition for you."

"Business?"

"Yeah, what do you think about turning this place

into a B&B?"

She shrugged her shoulders. "It's kind of small."

"We can add a bedroom and bathroom to the house and rent it out. Think about it—we're only five miles from the concert center. People will come from all over to be close to the venue. We could even put in a pool."

"Running a business like that is a lot of work."

"There you go again—always negative. That's probably why your ex-husband dumped you."

Dona's insides twisted. "My ex-husband didn't dump me."

"Don't worry about it," he snapped. "I'll find another way."

"How much do you need?"

"Five thousand should do it."

"That's a lot of money."

"It would cost a lot more if I hired someone to build it for us."

"Us?"

"We're getting old, Babe. We're going to need an income."

It was comforting to think they might grow old together for a moment.

"What if something happens to you? What if we break up?"

"That's not going to happen."

"Maybe you should sell the house," she said.

"Don't tell me what to do. You're just like every other woman I've known, trying to control my life."

"I'm not trying to control anyone's life."

"If you're not going to help me, you should go back to Florida." John was a stranger — his funny demeanor was replaced by an evil entity she didn't know or want to know. His eyes glittered with a savage rage. He slammed his cup of coffee down, spilling the liquid on the counter.

She could rationalize anything — anything except anger. A spark of adrenaline shot through Dona, and she couldn't hold back.

"I know all about your ex-girlfriend. She contacted me last week and warned me against you. She said all you wanted from me was money. Well, if money is why you asked me to come here, I'm done!" Dona snatched her keys and ran for the door.

John lunged for her — mouth twisted and eyes bright with anger. "Done? What's that supposed to mean?" He gripped her arm.

"You're hurting me. Let go." Dona yanked her arm from his grasp. "It means you're on your own. I'm leaving."

His demeanor changed.

"Calm down, Doll. That woman is just jealous because I love you and not her."

Dona tried to dismiss the alarm bells, but the message from Facebook was clear. She realized what he was up to now. Seeing his dark side, Dona wasn't blinded by passion. She resolved to leave, but his uncontrolled outbursts scared her. She had to outsmart him.

It was still dark outside the following day as she watched him pull out of the driveway. A steady rain was falling with no sign of stopping. John hadn't said goodbye before leaving for work. *Just as well! If he had, I might've changed my mind.*

Once his taillights disappeared, she grabbed the suitcase she had packed and ran to her car, tears trickling over her cheeks and mingling with the rain.

Light flashed across the angry sky as she backed out of the driveway. It illuminated the barn in her rearview mirror.

*"Stop! Go back!"* her heart cried. Maybe I misjudged him, she thought, trying to find any excuse to return. But pride propelled her forward.

"If you want to be happy with a man," her mother would say, "he has to love you more than you love him."

John would never love her as much as she loved him.

Driving down the main road, she passed the post office, the antique store, and the gas station as she skimmed several country blocks, then turned toward the route that would take her to the highway. Her car hit a large puddle, sending water over the windshield. Blinded for a moment, she gripped the steering wheel until her knuckles were white, then slammed on the brakes and pulled over to cry.

Dona felt her insides quiver. She tried to grasp the reality that he never really loved her. Feeling used, she navigated south, taking the quickest route home to Florida.

Halfway there, the phone rang. It was John. She let it go to voicemail and then pressed to hear the recording.

"Why did you leave me without an explanation?" His fury buzzed around the car like a swarm of bees. "And how dare you shut off the electricity? You're going to pay for this."

A knot formed in her gut. *Maybe I've made a mistake.*

As her car continued south, taking her further away from John, an overwhelming sense of loneliness gripped her. A familiar love song came on the radio. She didn't need reminding of what she never had, so she turned it off, but the melody remained in her head.

*Please, God, give me the strength to work through my pain and stand on my own two feet.*

# Chapter 32 | Rotten Apple

## *The Green Room*

---

Florida was just the way she had left it. The sun shone brightly, elevating her mood. She checked into a hotel and began the search for an apartment.

On the second day, she found a luxury apartment in the same town where her townhouse had been. It had a pool, tennis courts, and a clubhouse. Every month, they held a barbecue with live music. It was a typical cookie-cutter development where every unit looked the same. Dona had lived in places like that before, and it had never ended well. Before putting down a deposit, she decided to check one more place. It was an older apartment in the heart of the town. The complex was small and didn't have a pool, but it was nestled among restaurants and boutiques. There was even a park within walking distance. Dona called the property owner and scheduled a showing.

The two-bedroom unit on the second floor had a kitchen adjoining the living area, where large windows spanned the entire room. Sunshine poured in, filling the space with warmth. The first bedroom was small, but she thought it would make an excellent guest room. At the end of the hall was the main bedroom. It had a cathedral ceiling, more windows like the living room, and a walk-in closet. The best part was the beach, just two blocks away. *Who needs a pool?*

Dona accepted a position as a counselor at the community health center. Her specialty was codependency. She knew codependency inside and out but still struggled with her own anxieties. Still, she helped others overcome their fears. Dona knew firsthand — it wasn't always easy to leave abusive relationships. Fearing she might make another mistake, she swore off men. Mistakes — she made many of them in her life. But she pushed them aside until they were just bad memories.

\*\*\*\*\*

"Wake up!" Joe's voice sliced through the dark.

Dona jolted awake, disoriented. As the green walls came into focus, she felt disappointed to realize it wasn't just a nightmare. Seeing Joe's image on the screen, she wondered how long he had been staring at her. *Creepy!*

"Where were we?" he asked. He was losing patience with her. She could feel the atmosphere getting colder.

The daily questioning wore her down. She hated the way Joe manipulated her thoughts.

"Ah, yes," he said. "We were talking about love and relationships. You mentioned before that you wanted to be in love. If that's true, why do you resist committing to relationships?"

"I don't want to be accountable to anyone. Men expect too much and end up breeding discontent."

"So, you want to be alone, then?"

"I didn't exactly mean that. No one wants to be totally alone."

"Hmm. What if no one chooses to be with you in the future?" he asked, tugging on her insecurities.

"I guess that's a chance I'll have to take. If I ever decide to commit to a relationship, I will be the one to make the choice. In the past, I've let other people manipulate me. That's when I've made my biggest mistakes."

"Then, why date at all?"

"Well, sometimes I get lonely."

"One minute, you're lonely. Next, you want to be alone. I don't think you know what you want."

"I want to leave this room alive, you maniac! I want to block out your voice."

"You'll never do that! I will always be in your head."

The screen faded to black, but Dona didn't care.

Hunger made her glance at the door, searching for the tray. This time, it was a bowl of granola, a small container of skim milk, and an apple. It didn't interest her, but she suspected Joe was watching. She picked up the tray and brought it to the bed. The apple looked homegrown—all scrawny with brown spots. She wasn't crazy about apples. They reminded her of the fruit trees she'd planted in her yard when she lived in North Carolina—peach, cherry, and apple. The apples were messy. When they turned brown, they dropped from the trees, their cidery scent attracting flies and yellowjackets.

She took a bite of the apple anyway, but it left a foul taste in her mouth. She spat it out and reached for the water bottle, but it was empty.

She'd told Joe she wanted to be in love, but now, she doubted it. *If being in love means having someone control your life – no, thank you!*

Dona closed her eyes and let her mind float back to the past. For nearly a year after John, she was content to be on her own, finding her stride, developing skills, and gaining confidence. She began volunteering and made new friends – men and female alike. It was safer than dating.

Avoiding eye contact, Dona skirted around their proposals and managed to stay single for a while.

Sparked by the moon and stars outside her window, dreams of love returned. Her lonely soul yearned to find its other half.

# Chapter 33 | Trust

## *David*

---

Memories pulsed against the backs of her eyelids, and she remembered meeting David. She had become friends with two women who lived in her apartment building. They insisted on taking her to a lively Mexican eatery down the street.

"You should get out once in a while," Karen said. "Thursday night happy hour, two-for-one margaritas, and live music."

"All right. I could use a girls' night out."

Dona wore a black cotton sundress, which seemed perfect for a warm summer evening.

The music was loud, with young people crowding the bar, ready to soak up the bright lights and liquor. The place was jamming.

A good-looking man at the bar was also indulging in the two-for-one special. Surrounded by mostly females, he seemed to be well-liked.

Several stools at the bar were vacant, but Karen wanted a table. Dona noticed the man at the bar staring at her. He appeared to be in his mid-sixties—a wholesome, clean-looking man with broad shoulders, his dark hair streaked with gray.

When their eyes met, she looked down and blushed.

Debra sighed. "I don't believe I'll ever meet Mr. Right and get married."

"Love is a scam, anyway," Dona said. "If you put your faith in love, you're setting yourself up for disappointment."

"Don't listen to her," warned Karen. "She doesn't trust anyone."

"There's a reason for that," Dona defended, "in case you forgot."

"Love makes everything more meaningful," Debra insisted.

Karen downed the rest of her margarita and raised her hand to get the waitress's attention.

She laughed. "Dona's a magnet for men with issues."

"Give me your tired, your poor, your huddled masses… your down-and-outs. Yeah, I attract all the fixer-uppers."

Dona rarely made good choices when it came to men. She had a history of sympathizing with the underdogs of the world. Once she realized her mistake, her bleeding heart would erupt, leaving her standing in a puddle of her own making. It took some doing, but she always managed to unravel the web they tried to spin around her. But she made a lot of enemies along the way.

"I'd be happy without the games. I just want friends and good conversation. No stress, no pressure."

They all laughed as the musician, Dan Law, played his guitar, filling the room with a soulful rendition of *Midnight Rider*. His raspy voice had the women swooning and gyrating their hips to the music.

During the intermission, the man at the bar came over to their table.

"Is it all right if I join you?"

"Sure," Karen said, expecting him to sit in the empty chair next to her.

Instead, he pulled the chair next to Dona.

"I haven't seen you here before," he said.

"I'm not much of a bar person."

"I am—especially when they have bands. After working all week, I like to kick back a few and get lost in the blues."

"What do you do for a living?"

"I'm in real estate. I buy and sell houses."

"Oh. I used to be in real estate, but I lost my house."

David laughed. "That's funny."

"Now, I live in an apartment downtown. It's small, but I love it."

"At least you don't have to worry about maintenance and taxes."

"True. Since I enjoy traveling, I lock my door and take off. I just returned from Italy."

"You travel alone?"

"Yes. I usually do. I can do what I want when I want."

"That isn't very safe. You shouldn't take risks."

Dona laughed. "I'm not scared. It's been a while since I've been to Paris, and I always swore I'd return someday. Next trip, I'd like to go to Greece, but I haven't decided yet. Don't you like to travel?"

"I've never had the desire to leave the U.S. Besides, I'm somewhat of a workaholic."

"Is real estate that interesting?"

David frowned. "No, not really. I wanted to be a pilot. I planned to go to flight school, but my father was diagnosed with cancer. There was no way I could leave him."

"Did he know about your dream of becoming a pilot?"

"No, I never mentioned it, and then I met Libby. Once we were married, I gave up on flying."

"I'm sorry."

David shrugged. "It's okay. It's not too late. After our divorce, I signed up for flying lessons. I have one on Monday."

"That sounds exciting."

"Would you like to come along?"

"Me? Come with you?" Dona felt a panic attack coming on. She wasn't sure she was ready to date again after John, but David seemed so interesting.

"Yes, I love planes," she said.

"Great. In the meantime, let me cook dinner for you at my house on Saturday night. I live at the beach."

He was going a little too fast, but Dona didn't want to insult him. After all, it was only dinner.

"That would be lovely."

# Chapter 34 | Hardwood

## *David*

On Saturday morning, her son, Steven, called to say he would be coming for a visit in the spring. From the tone of his voice, Dona was sure Richard hadn't said anything. He was the only father Steven ever knew, and she hoped Richard would keep the secret and not punish him for her mistakes.

Dona offered him the guest room, but he said he'd rather stay at a hotel.

"We can meet for dinner," he said. "I'll formally introduce you to my fiancée."

"Fiancée? When did that happen?"

"We met at school and have been dating for almost a year. From the moment I met Samantha, I knew she was the one."

"I can't wait to meet her. I've also met someone. David's in real estate. He wants to cook dinner for me tonight, but I'm not sure if I should go."

"What are you afraid of?" Steven asked. "It's not as if you have to marry the guy."

"You're right, but maybe it's too soon."

Dona often fell headfirst into relationships without

a second thought. She didn't believe all men only wanted money or sex, but she still couldn't tell the good ones from the bad.

"Go. Have a little fun," he said. "I'll check him out when I get there." He laughed and added, "If he's still around, that is."

Dona hung up and sighed.

David seemed like a generous and good-hearted man. Too good to be true. She wondered why some other woman hadn't already snatched him up.

After a shower, she felt better about going out. Wearing tight white jeans and a black spaghetti-strapped top, she slipped into her black high-heeled shoes. *Not bad for an old broad!*

She jotted down the directions to David's house on a Post-it note.

*****

Dona drove out of her gate and followed the directions, turning left onto a narrow road that ran along the beach. David's house was extraordinary. The front entrance had double French doors, with palm trees etched into the sidelights. The scent of jasmine followed her with every step. The door opened before she rang the bell.

"Welcome to my humble abode," David said.

"Humble? This looks like a scene from *Gone with the Wind!*"She said, awed by the opulence.

"If you don't mind, please take off your shoes and leave them by the door."

"Shrrre." Dona looked at her feet and giggled. "Are you a germaphobe?"

"Yes, but that's not why. The heels scratch up the hardwood floors. Come on in," David said with a chuckle, leading her to the living room.

Sliding glass doors formed the walls, allowing a full ocean view. David opened one, and the salty air whisked in, blowing back her hair. Amused by her wide-eyed wonderment, he grabbed her arm and pulled her out onto the balcony.

"Wow... is that your boat?"

"Yes, I like to go fishing at least once or twice a month. It relaxes me. Do you like fishing?"

"Yes, as long as someone else baits the hook."

David laughed. "Would you like to go out on the boat next weekend? You could lie on the stern and take in the sun."

"I'd love to."

For a moment, they stood listening to the waves as they crashed upon the shore. A warm breeze enveloped her.

"This is so beautiful."

David nodded. "That's why I bought this house. Seeing you with the wind in your hair and wearing that outfit, I want to kiss you." Without another word, he wrapped his arms around her and kissed her until her knees grew weak.

"Come on. I'll show you around." In a half-daze, Dona let him lead her to a massive kitchen. He opened the pantry door and removed an apron from the hook on the back.

"I love to cook," he said, pulling out a sharp knife to cut the chicken.

"I can tell you know your way around a kitchen. Can I help?"

"No. Relax. I've got it all under control. I did all the cooking when I was married to my ex, Libby. She wasn't good at it, although she tried. Finally, I insisted on taking over the job."

"I did all the cooking in my family," she said. "The kitchen was my domain. I loved to bake. I'd pull out the flour and whip up some cookies whenever stressed. Unfortunately, those days are gone. Lately, I've been forgetting ingredients, such as sugar in cookies or baking powder in muffins. Everything is either burnt or raw. My timing is off, so I avoid the oven.

He smiled and lined the glass casserole pan with potatoes, chopped onion, and chicken. Last, he opened a can of tomatoes, poured them on the chicken, and then covered the pan with aluminum foil.

"Voila," he said, popping the pan into a preheated oven. "Dinner will be ready in about an hour."

"Can I help you set the table?"

"It's already set."

David led her back into the living room and motioned for her to sit while he mixed two dirty martinis at the bar, then sat beside her.

"So, how long were you married?" he asked.

"Twenty years. I never counted on divorce, but things happen."

"I know what you mean. Libby was the one who

wanted to split. She claimed I was domineering."

"What does that mean?"

"Well, it's true. I was a little anal then, but I've mellowed out since. Some things aren't as important anymore. I learned that lesson after my father was diagnosed with cancer."

His eyes drifted off to a faraway place. Dona's heart ached for him, but she didn't know what to say. Saved by the kitchen timer, David brought the casserole to the table. Before lighting the candles, he poured the wine and dimmed the lights. He created a romantic ambiance.

Awkward silence always made her feel like she had to fill in the gaps, and she disclosed more than she intended. Later, she'd chastise herself for exposing her innermost feelings. Dona learned the hard way to keep her mouth shut.

Listening intently to David's stories, she took small bites of food. Usually, she was an open book and did all the talking. She wore her heart on her sleeve and said whatever popped into her head.

After dinner, they returned to the living room and sat on the couch. David moved closer. She felt his body heat. Without warning, he pressed his lips against hers. She closed her eyes, enjoying the passionate kisses until his hands wandered up the back of her shirt. Dona froze. She wanted to kick herself for being such a prude, but he was going too fast.

"I'm sorry," he said, sensing her uneasiness. "I didn't mean to come on so strong. It's just that you're so beautiful."

"Thanks," she said, feeling uncomfortable. Standing at the top of his pedestal seemed like a long way down. It was dizzying.

David kept his distance for a while, but it wasn't long before he reached out again, touching her hair, rubbing her leg, holding her hand, all seemingly innocent.

"I should be going." She stood up to leave. "I have to get up early for work tomorrow."

"Maybe we can do this again," he suggested.

"We'll see."

"What's the matter? Didn't you like my cooking?"

"Yes, of course. You're a fantastic cook."

David walked her to her car and looked into her eyes before giving her a long, good-night kiss.

"I really shouldn't let you leave," he said. "You've had a few glasses of wine."

"Don't worry."

"I don't want you to get stopped by the police."

"I'm fine."

"Take the back roads."

"Okay, Daddy!"

"Call me Poppy!"

"I'm a big girl, Poppy. I can find my way home."

He smiled. "Don't forget, Monday we're flying. I'll pick you up around five."

"Why so early?"

"It takes time to prepare a flight schedule, and I like to watch the sunrise while they do the paperwork."

It felt good to have someone in her life again.

David was everything she wanted in a man: thoughtful and accomplished. However, he seemed to be a little too controlling, in a caring way.

She recalled her first time on David's boat. She had stuck her hand out to touch the force of the wind. A showering mist hit her face as they glided through the water. It made her feel free as the boat skimmed across the ocean, as if she were flying. It was a perfect day, except for the boat shoes he made her wear. David had insisted on them so she wouldn't fall overboard.

The boat curved around at top speed, and she held on tight. It sped toward an island up ahead, where he had planned a picnic. She could still hear the squawk of the seagulls swooping over them in search of fish as they ate sandwiches and potato salad. She loved the feel of the sand between her toes as they walked on the beach and the cool blue water afterward when they took a swim.

"Don't go out too far," he warned, "you could get caught in the undertow."

"Don't be such a worry-wart." Dona smiled and dove into the waves.

# Chapter 35 | Flying High

## David

On Monday morning, David pulled into her driveway with his black hair windblown, the Porsche's top down.

Dona slid into the soft leather seat of his Porsche. He sped along the highway with the music blaring, and neither of them spoke. *I could get used to this,* she thought.

"There's a restaurant at the edge of the runway," David said. "It has a great view, and we can have something to eat while we watch the planes take off."

David directed her to a booth in the far corner. The sun peeked over the horizon, painting a sky of orange, pink, and blue.

"This is the best spot to see the planes take off," he said, signaling for the waitress.

A slightly overweight woman in her late thirties rushed over.

"Hi, Davie," she said flirtatiously.

"You look lovely today, Rachel. Did you cut your hair?"

She ran her fingers through her bangs. "Yeah, I did

it myself. It's uneven."

"You look great. This is Dona," he said, introducing them."

"Hi, Dona. It's nice to meet you."

Dona smiled. "It's nice to meet you, too."

"You have a good man here. If I weren't already married, I'd snatch him up."

"Don't listen to her, Dona. She had her chance and blew it."

Rachel laughed. "So, what can I get for you folks?"

"I'll have two eggs over easy and a coffee," David said. "How about you, Dona?"

"I'm probably better off with an empty stomach while we're in the air. I'll just have coffee — two creams, no sugar, please."

"You have to eat something," he insisted.

"I'm too nervous to eat."

"At least have some toast."

"All right," she relented.

"Coming right up." Rachel walked away, tugging on the hem of her uniform, which had crept well up her thighs.

They stared out the window as a plane glided in for a landing.

"Boy, I'd love to have one of those," he said.

"What kind of plane is that?"

"A Cirrus SR22. It has a 310-horsepower engine." He pointed out the window. "Keep your eye on that red-tipped plane out there. There's my instructor. He stood up and threw a twenty-dollar bill on the table. "Are you ready?"

"I think so."

"Don't be scared. The instructor will take charge if anything goes wrong."

Dona followed David out onto the runway, and they climbed into the cockpit.

"This is my girlfriend, Dona. She'll be flying with us today."

"The instructor shook her hand. "Glad you can join us, Dona." He secured her seatbelt and turned his attention to the instrument panel. After radioing the air tower, they received clearance to taxi. The plane raced down the runway, giving Dona a surge of adrenaline. She held her breath and closed her eyes as they lifted off. She looked out at a beautiful, clear blue sky when she opened them again. As her heart rate stabilized, she began to relax. She felt as free as a bird.

When the plane landed, they stepped down to the ground, and David scooped her up in his arms, his eyes full of life.

"That was exhilarating," he shouted over the plane's engines.

"Yes, it certainly was," she said. Dona was thrilled to be sharing the moment with him.

"Let's have lunch," he said, linking his arm in hers.

"Yes, and a bottle of wine," she added.

"Or two," he said, laughing.

The attraction between them was electrifying, and by the end of the day, Dona found herself back at his house. David poured wine and loaded a CD into the player. After a few glasses of wine, all her inhibitions seemed to disappear. He kissed her neck while caressing her breast. She didn't stop him.

"Let's take a bath in my Jacuzzi. You'll love it."

A bath meant getting naked. This time, she knew she would have to sleep with him. Dona didn't want him to think she was leading him on, so she had difficulty saying no.

He led her into the bathroom. He set his glass of wine down, then turned on the faucet and poured Jasmine bath oil into the water, filling the room with a sweet aroma. Then he lit some candles. "I'm a romantic guy. What can I say?"

Dona tried not to roll her eyes. That was something John always claimed. Usually, when a man said he was romantic, it was a recipe for disappointment and disaster.

The candles flickered, lighting the corners of the room, and soft music set the mood. David kissed her and wrapped his arms around her waist, pulling her closer. He pushed the straps of her sundress off her shoulders. Unclasping her bra, it fell to the floor, along with her panties, leaving her exposed. She crossed her arms over her chest.

David moved them away. "They're perfect, just like you." He kissed her right breast, sending a shiver of pleasure up and down her spine. He repeated the kiss on her left breast. As he pulled his t-shirt over his head, she noticed the outlines of his muscles. It was evident he spent a lot of time in the gym. David wasn't your typical beer-guzzling sixty-something-year-old.

He slid off his pants, dropped his boxer shorts, and slipped into the steamy water.

"Get in," he coaxed with a lecherous grin.

Dona eased into the bubbly liquid, and David pulled her between his legs and soaped her back. He nuzzled her neck.

Sipping their wine, they lay back and listened to the sounds of Harry Belafonte. After finishing the bottle, they ended up in bed. Dona remembered floating as he carried her up the stairs.

David was an attentive lover and whispered adoring words while they made love, but she was tense.

Afterward, she breathed in his scent and sighed, realizing how lonely she'd been.

"Spend the night," he whispered. "We're just getting started."

*Just?* She panicked.

"Sorry, David, I need to get home. I have to work tomorrow."

"I can't get enough of you," he said, looking disappointed.

"Maybe next time," she placated. Tempted to bask in his attention, she almost gave in. Before he could change her mind, she slipped out of bed and went downstairs to get dressed.

David stepped into his pants and walked her out to the car. "I wish you would stay," he pleaded and puckered his lips.

She laughed and gently pulled free. "It's better to sleep in my own bed tonight. I'll talk to you in the morning," she said and drove away.

# Chapter 36 | Whirlwind

## *David*

Dona hadn't planned to get into another relationship, but David was persistent, always tempting her with fun things to do or delicious dinners.

On the weekends, they went sailing on his boat. Sometimes, they caught fish, and David cooked them for dinner. Drinking fine wines and listening to music, she settled into the relationship.

"Next week, you should come to my house for dinner," she said. "I'll make you an Italian dish."

"That sounds great, but I can't eat tomato sauce. It repeats on me. Maybe it's the garlic."

"Hmm. Okay, then I'll grill us a steak."

David's face contorted.

"Don't tell me," she said. "You don't eat meat."

"I eat chicken," he said with a smile.

"How about clams and linguine? That's Italian."

"I love clams and linguine."

All right, then. I'll make that. Do you have any other food phobias?"

"I don't think so."

"Good. After dinner, we can walk around town. It will be fun."

The following weekend, Dona pulled out all the stops. A crusty loaf of Italian bread was heating in the oven while she made a special salad, slicing the lettuce into strips and arranging cucumbers, tomato, olives, salami, and cheese on each plate. She bought two baked clams on the half-shell and fresh littleneck clams to add to the broth and pour over the linguine.

David seemed to enjoy it. However, he suggested that the next time she shouldn't add too much garlic and perhaps add a splash of red pepper.

Dona felt deflated. It was her mother's recipe, and no one had ever complained about it.

"Next time, I'll make the clam sauce," he said.

The sky grew cloudy by the time they finished eating, threatening their walk.

"I think it's going to rain," he said. "Maybe we should stay in and watch television."

"Don't be silly. I checked the forecast, and there's only a forty percent chance. Besides, a little rain won't kill us."

"All right."

"Great. I just need to grab my phone."

Dona noticed two missed calls and saw that her phone was on silent mode. *Hmm.* She pursed her lips. *I don't remember doing that.*

"Is everything all right?" David asked.

Dona smiled and shook it off.

"Yes. Let's go."

Holding hands, they walked through the streets, stopping to listen to live music from one of the bars. As they passed the park, Dona nudged him. "Let's swing on the swings."

"The sign says it closes at dusk. If there are any cops around, we may get in trouble."

Dona laughed. "What are they going to do, arrest us?"

He gave her a sheepish smile. "All right. Let's do it."

They climbed the gate and ran around the park like children, laughing so hard that their sides hurt.

As they walked back to her apartment, the sky opened. Ducking under an awning, David kissed her. It was very romantic—just like a movie. He looked adoringly into her eyes and whispered, "I love you."

"I love you too," Dona said, but it didn't feel like the same love she had felt for John—that obsessive, aching love that nearly killed her. Swept into his euphoria, she went along for the ride.

David introduced her to his friends. He gushed about how wonderful she was and that *she* was *the one!*

Before she knew it, they were visiting his mother at her nursing home in Rhode Island. She was as wonderful as he said, and so were his sisters. Dona was immediately part of the family and saddled with all the responsibilities that go with it. It was difficult to navigate one person's feelings, but now, she had to ensure she didn't disappoint the whole clan. The pressure was on.

At his house, they watched funny movies and

laughed uproariously.

"I love your feet," he said while they were watching one of his favorites, *My Big Fat Greek Wedding*. He had seen it a million times, but he loved to laugh.

"I have a foot fetish," he said and lifted her foot.

Dona giggled and wriggled out of his grasp. "That's weird."

His admiration was excessive. He loved her eyes, her hair, her legs, and he even loved her protruding belly. Dona was flattered, but she wondered if he truly saw her or if she was a projection of some idealized image in his mind.

"We're meant for each other," he said.

"Realistically—we don't know if we'll be together forever."

"I love you." He stroked her hair.

"Sooner or later, the reality will set in, and I may shatter your expectations."

"That's not going to happen. I'm so lucky to have you in my life. I'm never going to let you go."

Dona laughed. "What if I disappeared?"

"I'd hunt you down—even if I have to go to the end of the earth."

"Things happen. Relationships don't always work out."

"This one will," he insisted. "You make me happy."

"If you're looking to me to make you happy, you may be disappointed. I don't have that kind of power. I can make you smile, but I can't make you happy."

"You do make me happy. I don't want to live without you."

"That's crazy talk." She wanted to think he was kidding, but it concerned her.

David could not be ignored — flowers, love notes, home-cooked dinners, and wine. They both loved going to the beach, napping under an umbrella, and only getting up to frolic in the ocean and cool off. The beach was a smorgasbord to David. He couldn't get enough of the pretty girls who strolled by in their bikinis. Dona followed his gaze to a woman in her early thirties. He focused his attention on her. Even though it was excessive, she glossed over it. It felt good to have someone who loved her.

"I guess you find her attractive," she said, snapping him back to reality.

He smiled sheepishly. "She does have a nice body, but I prefer yours." He reached over and ran his hand over her thigh, moving dangerously close to her crotch.

"Hey! We're in a public place." Dona pushed his hand away.

"No one is looking," he said. "You're delectable — so soft and tanned."

There was always a sexual expectation to his praise, making her uncomfortable. After a long day of sun and surf, Dona packed her towel and sunscreen to go home.

"Come back to my house," David said. "I'll cook dinner. Besides, I have something important to discuss with you."

"What is it?"

"Nothing bad, I assure you."

Before they left the beach, David washed off the chairs and the umbrella.

"Make sure to rinse your feet," he reminded. "I don't want sand in the car."

"It's only sand," she said. "We live in Florida. There's always sand in my car."

David laughed. "Yeah. You seem to take the beach with you wherever you go."

Dona rolled her eyes. She couldn't imagine worrying about things so trivial.

They went back to David's house, and Dona took a shower. At his insistence, she'd left clothes at his place. She thought it was odd and didn't want to part with her clothing. She only left items she wouldn't miss if they were lost. She stood under the showerhead for a long time, letting the warm water flow over her, then slipped into an old sundress and went downstairs to the patio, where David was sitting. He was already sipping a glass of wine on the terrace and seemed lost in his thoughts.

"Sorry it took me so long," she said.

"That's all right," he said, handing her a glass of merlot.

David waited for her to take a few sips, then took the glass and set it on the table.

"Dinner smells wonderful," she said.

Before they sat down, Dona's phone chimed with a text.

David's brows knotted above his eyes. "Your phone rings constantly. Can you shut it?"

"Shut it? What if it's important?"

"At least put it on silent mode. Only while we're eating."

"All right," she said reluctantly. She would never make such a request.

Dona was as quiet as her phone during dinner.

As David cleared the dishes, she stared out the window. The awkward silence made her uncomfortable.

"It's so nice out," she said in an attempt to fix the situation. "Can we go for a walk?"

"I guess you can persuade me… as long as you let me have my way with you when we get back."

As they strolled along the shoreline, the salty air relaxed her.

David took her hand as they walked on the sand, and then his hand gently gripped the back of her neck. It wasn't easy being connected to someone while they were walking. She felt restrained and pulled away.

"Let's go back home and make love," he said. "We can tell each other everything that matters in the world."

"Ten more minutes. I love the sound of the ocean."

"You know — you could have this every day."

"How so?"

"You could move in with me."

"I'm not sure that's a good idea. We've only been together a few months."

"Yeah, but we get along so well. Wouldn't it be nice to wake up together every morning? You know I love you, don't you?"

"I love you, too," she responded. "But..." she wasn't sure.

"I don't want to make a mistake. I need more time."

"I understand. I just want you to know. It's always an option."

"I do. Thank you, but I'm not ready."

David's offer to move in was tempting. Generous and caring, he knew how to treat a woman with respect. He would have made a great husband if they had met twenty-five years earlier. He could take good care of her, and she wouldn't be alone. He had the best of everything, but material things had no value to Dona. After losing everything following her divorce, she realized that things didn't make someone happy. She'd have to give up her independence. Besides, he was overly nurturing. The cost was too high.

David finally accepted the arrangement. Yet, every so often, his insecurity about the future showed. He was falling into a depression. His melancholy demeanor hung over her head like a guillotine. Feeling selfish, she distanced herself. She couldn't afford to have his desperation pull her down.

Dona tried to break up with him several times, but it always made her feel like she'd kicked a puppy. It wasn't fair.

He insisted they could remain friends, and she couldn't say no.

# Chapter 37 | Down the Drain

## The Green Room

---

Dona looked across the room and spotted another tray by the door. *Was it there all the while?* They appeared and disappeared like magic. She wondered why the sound didn't wake her when he returned to retrieve them. Everything suddenly became clear. Joe was drugging her. That's why she was always tired.

Terrified, she realized that was how he entered the room to collect the trays without her seeing. His anger scared her. She wasn't sure what heinous acts he was capable of. *He could rape me. Or even kill me.*

Trapped like a rabbit in a snare, she wasn't ready to accept her fate. She needed to outsmart him.

*From now on, I'll pour the beverages down the drain!*

Breakfast was toast, scrambled eggs, and coffee. Dona ate the food but poured the coffee into the toilet. She didn't need a morning nap, which confirmed the theory of being drugged. As Dona's head cleared, she had a heightened sense of awareness.

Joe appeared on the screen. This time, he didn't catch her by surprise. Sitting on the edge of the bed, she folded her arms across her chest. She met his eyes and glared.

"Good morning," Joe said. If he noticed that she wasn't sleeping, he didn't mention it.

Dona wanted to confront him and tell him exactly what she thought, but fear kept her mouth shut.

"Are you up for some questions, Dona?"

"What do you hope to gain by keeping me a prisoner here?"

Joe's eyes widened. "I'm the one asking the questions. Did you forget?"

"I think it's only fair that you answer mine. After all, I've been very cooperative."

"This is true. All right, let's do this. I'll let you ask me one for every question you answer."

Dona bit her lip and thought about the psychology behind that. It reminded her of John. Every time he gave her something, it lulled her into a state of passivity. Then, soon after, he took more than he gave.

"Okay, but you must answer my questions honestly. I'll have to be firm about that."

Joe laughed. "You have many qualities, Dona, but you couldn't be firm if your life depended on it."

"At least give me a chance."

"Okay. I would like to revisit the topic of your relationship aversion. What exactly do you like about living alone?"

"Independence. I can do what I want when I want and not feel guilty."

"Is that why you don't want to live with a man?"

"It's not that. I never really had the chance to be on my own. Deep down, I guess I was looking forward to it."

"What about love?"

"I believe it's my turn."

Joe laughed. "Shoot!"

She thought she heard a tinge of a southern accent. Dona tried to think of something that might reveal his identity.

"Have you lived in the mountains all of your life?"

"Did I say we were in the mountains?"

"Are we in a large town?"

"That's two questions. You still haven't explained why you want to live alone."

"Don't you have any value for love?"

"There are more important things than love," she said.

"Like?"

"Like peace of mind...like contentment."

"Don't you worry that you'll end up lonely?"

His question shook her to the core. Dona did want love, but she also wanted to be independent. Maybe she couldn't have both. Still, she tried to hang onto relationships, even if they weren't right. She feared being abandoned. She had wondered if abandoned was the right word, so she looked it up in the dictionary.

Abandon means to give up or discontinue any further interest in something because of discouragement, weariness, distaste, or the like: to abandon one's efforts.

Yes, abandon was the right word.

"That's three questions," she said, avoiding the

answer. It's my turn."

"Are you from the south?"

"I know what you're up to, and it won't work," he bellowed. "Who do you think you are, Missy? If you persist, we'll have to continue this later." The screen turned black.

"I'm sorry!" Dona blurted. "Please, I'm sorry. I don't want to go back to the basement.

He ignored her pleas. She dropped her head into her hands and sobbed.

Dinner consisted of a hot dog, beans, chocolate pudding, and iced tea—no coffee. She poured the drink down the drain and ate the pudding. At least she'd have a chance to fight if she weren't drugged.

After twenty minutes, her eyelids grew heavy, and her head spun. *The pudding!* Dona fought to stay awake. Drifting in and out of consciousness, she thought she saw the silhouette of a man hovering over her. The image shattered like glass falling onto a hard floor. Sinking into a nightmare, she dreamed she wasn't alone. She dreamed that she was spooning. At first, she thought it was David, but when she turned to look at him, it was Joe. Waking in a cold sweat, the scent of a man filled the room.

She looked around, sensing a presence in the room. Her arm flung out to the side. No one was there, but the sheets were warm. She rolled over to look. The covers were in disarray, and the imprint of someone had dented the mattress. It horrified her to know Joe might have been there.

Her palms were damp, and she couldn't stop her

body from shaking. With a sudden burst, her anger turned to resolve. Dona knew what she had to do. She had to fight back.

A new food tray was in front of the door, but she decided it wasn't safe to eat.

It wasn't long before Joe realized what she was doing.

"Why aren't you eating?" he asked. "Are you trying to make yourself sick?"

"I'd rather starve to death than spend another day in this room, listening to your voice."

"But we're getting along so well." Joe laughed.

His laughter sparked a surge of adrenaline in her, and she couldn't let him win so easily.

"Screw you!" she murmured, forgetting her fear that he may hurt her.

"What did you say?"

"I said that's a matter of perception," Dona replied, her voice more restrained as she bent to his will.

He wasn't torturing her physically — so far, but psychologically, she was a mess. *I'm safe, but for how long?*

Dona refused to eat or drink, even when he tempted her with coffee and tasty meals. Water from the tap was her only source of nutrition. It tasted like sulfur, but she took small sips.

At first, her stomach growled and burned. Her senses sharpened as her body adjusted to starvation, but it didn't stop the memories from rolling around in her head. Joe was still in control.

# Chapter 38 | Acceptance

### *David*

---

*Maybe I should have stayed with David. At least he loved me.* Dona thought about the ocean breeze filtering through his bedroom, but then remembered why she couldn't be with him. His love and concern were reassuring, although stifling. She recalled a conversation they had about her travels.

"I'm thinking of going to Paris in the spring," she said.

"Didn't you just go to Europe?"

"Yes, but I feel the urge for some Old World culture."

"Spring is my busy season. I can't take off from work."

"Oh! I'll have to go by myself."

David frowned. "It's dangerous for a woman traveling alone. You could get kidnapped or taken advantage of by some suave Frenchman."

"Don't be silly. I always travel alone. I admit I've had a few close calls, but I can take care of myself."

"What if I don't want you to go?"

"Then we'd have a problem." The predicament

she landed in was the very one she had set out to avoid.

"Maybe I'll call my cousin. She's usually up for a spur-of-the-moment trip."

"I don't want anything bad to happen to you." He lifted her face and tried to kiss her, but she turned her head away.

They would have been good together. *If only he weren't such a mother hen.*

Dona couldn't do the things she always did without putting it past him first. David wanted to know where she was at all times — for her own safety. She couldn't even go out with her girlfriends for a social evening and a drink because he claimed it was inviting trouble. Dona began holding back information. One night, she joined her friends for a quick drink. She wouldn't have felt the need to hide it from him if he weren't such a worrywart.

Leaving her phone in the car, she had only planned to stay an hour or two, but had so much fun that she stayed until the bar closed. When she checked her cellphone, there were four missed calls and five texts from David.

The next day, she listened as he gave her the third degree.

"I'm sorry," she said. "My phone was dead, and I put it on the charger. I guess I forgot about it."

Overwhelmed by a push-pull reaction, she tried to reconcile her feelings. David was her best friend. She enjoyed spending time with him, fishing, listening to music, and having their dinners together. At night, they took long walks or watched a movie on television.

David saw her doubt. She had plenty. They gnawed at her, but Dona couldn't pin them down. She tried to shove them to the back of her mind to deal with it later. They peeked out from time to time and then quickly receded before she could react. She and David were unraveling at an alarming rate, and she started to feel his animosity.

"It's been a long day," she said. "I think I'll go home early."

"I don't understand why you won't move in with me."

"David, I told you, I don't want to live with you. I need to be independent. Besides, I'm not going to leave my apartment. I'm perfectly happy there."

"When you say that, I think it's the beginning of the end, my love," he said, tugging her insecurities.

"That's silly," Dona said, but took a pause. Her bottom lip trembled. Maybe he sensed something amiss.

She had no desire for marriage. *Been there, done that!*

"I was married for twenty years, and part of the reason I stayed was that I feared being on my own. I need to come to grips with that first."

"I understand, but I don't want to lose you."

"I'm trying to figure things out between us. It doesn't seem so easy anymore."

"Is it because of your ex-husband? Is he still trying to get you back?"

"I haven't heard from Richard in months."

"But he knows where you live. He has your

address."

"Yeah, that's where he sends my alimony. Why?"

"Maybe Richard still loves you."

"That's ridiculous. Any relationship I had with Richard is over. As long as he sends the check every month, I don't need to talk to him. And it's always on time."

"I was just wondering."

"You can't keep trying to figure out what's in my head. I need a little space."

As they sat silently watching a documentary about Anthony Bourdain, he jumped up and went to the bedroom. When he returned, something was in his eyes — a desperation that scared her.

"I don't think you know what you want," he snapped. "I think you should go home now, Dona." He grabbed her purse and escorted her to the door. She had never seen him that angry and drove home, feeling numb. *Is he just like the others?*

She took a long walk around town, her mind racing. She had so many questions, but the answers were clear to her. She couldn't give David what he wanted — for her to fold neatly into his life. She needed her freedom. It was a tough decision, but Dona was tired of holding onto a relationship that didn't work. *It's time to end it.*

The thought of being alone again shook her. She felt as if there was a hole in her life.

After moping around for a week, she made an appointment to see a therapist.

"Why do I feel so empty?" Dona asked.

"You're mourning the relationship," the therapist said. "It's called the stages of grief."

"But I wanted to break up with him."

"Habits aren't easy to end. You spent a great deal of time with this man. There will be times when you miss his company."

"Lately, I can't breathe. I'm either holding my breath or hyperventilating. What is that?"

"Anxiety, but you can learn to control that."

"How?"

"Relax and take deep breaths through your nose, filling your abdomen. Hold it for a few seconds, and then release it slowly from your mouth. Remember, the feeling is only temporary. Try to keep busy. Live in the now. You will only magnify your regrets by looking back. You can't change the past. By the same token, if you worry about the future, you are stressing about things that haven't even happened or may never happen."

"You're right, of course. Looking back, I think about what I could have done differently. When I look forward, I worry that David may hate me."

"He might. He's also going through the stages of grief. If he can't get to the acceptance stage, he may turn his anger against you."

# Chapter 39 | Common Thread

## The Green Room

---

Dona lay on the bed and stared at the Styrofoam ceiling tiles, the only part of the room that wasn't green. A lifetime of struggle flooded her mind.

After the divorce, she took her freedom for granted and hopped from one man to another. Now, she realized that all her relationships were prisons of one type or another, but they had no visible bars. Like an electric fence, she feared stepping over to the other side. It was as if her ability to detach had been conditioned out.

Dona had poor taste in men—starting with Angelo. Jealous and possessive. She moved in with Angelo at eighteen to leave her childhood home. He made all the decisions—what movies to see, what restaurants to eat at, and who her friends were. Eventually, he tried to dictate everything, from what she could wear to when her family could visit.

She married Richard, hoping he would give her a family life and security. She spent two decades believing that her way of life felt secure, but it was hanging by a thread. She stayed in the marriage and turned a blind eye to his cheating because she was afraid to let go. The house kept her happy for a while. She could see past the worn-out siding and peeling paint, always envisioning how magnificent the house could be — if only he had finished it.

Dona thought she might have learned the signs from her psychology classes, but love blinded her from seeing that John was a sociopath. He never really loved her. When she first met John, she thought she had found the love of her life. They seemed to be on the same wavelength, but he played a psychological game, and she was an easy target.

She wanted John to love her. At the time, she thought money was important, but what did it matter? *Maybe I should have given all my money to John.*

Then she turned to David to take away her loneliness. At first, his embrace was warm and secure. All the attention was flattering. He promised to improve everything, but he also wanted to be with her all the time. Afraid to make him mad, she tried to juggle her needs and his, failing miserably. She had no time for herself, and it was suffocating.

What did they all have in common?

All her life, passive-aggressive men threw her into a crazy, repetitive Groundhog Day.

She ruminated over and over for answers that simply weren't there. In retrospect, she saw that their manipulation fueled her behaviors. As soon as she sensed their control, she bolted. They wanted something from her that she couldn't give them. They eventually became angry, which Dona couldn't handle.

Anger always triggered her into a people-pleasing mode. She suspected it all started with her father. Always seeking his approval and coming up short, she went above and beyond to please him. *Any child of an alcoholic father is going to be damaged.* Her greatest fear was that he would abandon her if she disappointed him. She contemplated her fucked-upness!

*Maybe that's why I'm in this green prison.*

Dona thought of all the things she would do when she got out—if she got out. She felt a shift in her mindset and realized she must change. She wanted to find the source of fortitude within herself—to exist without relying on another person for emotional nourishment. *If I ever get free, I won't let anyone manipulate me again. I will do what I want, rather than going along to get along.*

*Surely, someone will realize I'm missing. My son? My ex-husband? No. The only person who cares enough to miss me is....*

# Chapter 40 | Missing

### *David*

---

Two weeks earlier, David tried to call Dona again. "The party that you are trying to reach is unavailable. Please leave a message after the beep."

"Dammit!" He left another message. "Dona, call me—no matter what time it is."

He backed out of his driveway, mashed the gas pedal, and headed to her apartment, growing angrier with each mile. Dona's parking spot was vacant. He looked up at her window. No lights were on. *Maybe she's asleep.*

Just in case, he rummaged through his glove compartment for the key he had taken and forgotten to put back on the hook after he brought out the trash. Manuals and random paperwork spilled out. There it was, under them.

First, David knocked. Then he knocked louder. He unlocked the door and entered the apartment. The switch on the wall was illuminated by the solar panel, and he flipped it on. The stillness of the air and the closed blinds confirmed she wasn't there.

"Dona?" he whispered, heading down the hallway

to her bedroom. The covers were neatly tucked, and there was no sign that she had slept there.

After checking the living room and kitchen, he remembered she sometimes worked late. He locked the door and drove to her office building.

David counted to the fourth-floor window, but it was dark. No one was working late. He drove home and paced back and forth in his room, wearing a path on the carpet. One more time, he thought. Dialing Dona's phone, he left a message.

David slipped off his shoes and lay on the bed with his eyes closed, waiting for the phone to ring. An hour passed, and he pulled the covers up to his chin over his fully clothed body. The sound of the ocean waves drifted through the sliding glass doors. He concentrated on their rhythm, waiting for them to soothe him to drift off to sleep. His mind wouldn't let him rest. Fitfully dozing, he woke periodically to look at the clock.

After tossing and turning all night, he tried to call Dona in the morning. "We're sorry. The mailbox of the person you are trying to reach is full."

Frustrated, he called her office. "Is Dona Pearson there?"

"No, she hasn't come in for a few days," the receptionist said.

"Can you call me if you hear from her?"

"Yes, of course."

David gave her his number, then hung up and dialed 911. "I want to report a missing person."

"Are you next of kin?"

"She's my girlfriend," David said impatiently.

"So, you aren't her next of kin?"

"She's my fiancée," he snapped.

"Oh! How long has she been missing?"

"I'm not sure. Dona hasn't shown up for work in a few days."

"Maybe she's visiting someone."

"No, I would know that. She's missing."

"Sir, we see this kind of thing all the time."

"What if she's hurt?"

"I'm sure she's just fine," the officer tried to reassure him. "Try calling her family and friends. Call us back if you don't hear from her in a few days."

David hung up and called Dona's son, Steven. "Have you heard from your mother today?"

"No, we haven't spoken in over a week," he said. "Is something wrong?"

"I've been trying to call her, but she doesn't answer. I'm worried. It's my fault," David moaned. "I was pressuring her to move in with me."

"I'm sure she wouldn't leave because of that."

"Maybe she's with my grandmother. I'll call and get back to you."

"Thanks," David said. He hung up and waited.

Thirty minutes passed, but it felt like an hour. David jumped when the phone rang.

"Hi, David. This is Steven."

"Did you find her?"

"No, my grandmother hasn't heard from her. I also called my aunt Julie. She hasn't heard from her either. Richie is out of the country, so I'm unable to contact him. Now I'm worried, too."

"What about your father?"

"I tried, but he didn't answer. I'll call him again. Did you call the police?"

"Yes, but they won't do anything until tomorrow."

"I'll call you if I hear from her," Steven said.

"Okay, I'll keep looking. Let me know if you get any leads." David refused to wait for the police. He drove around town to all the places she might have gone. He checked the gym, the mall, the supermarket, and even the beach, desperate to find her.

*****

Twenty-four hours went by, and there was still no sign of Dona. David's cellphone rang, and Steven's name came up.

"Did you hear from your mother?" he practically begged.

"No, I tried to leave a message, but her mailbox is full. Maybe you should call the police again."

David hung up and called the station. "I want to report a missing person."

"Child or adult?"

"An adult—female," he said impatiently.

"How long has she been missing?"

"A week, damn it!"

"Calm down, sir. Give me your address. I'll send an officer to make the report."

"158 Ocean Drive...."

"Someone will be there shortly."

David hung up and opened the patio sliding doors. He could see white foam cresting the waves in the moonlight. The ocean roared, waves crashing angrily against the shore. Thirty minutes later, he heard a knock at the front door. The officer was a female in her early thirties.

"Hello, sir," she said stiffly. "You called about a missing person? I'm here to take a report."

"Yes, my girlfr... eh, fiancée is missing. I think she may be hurt."

"What makes you think that? Did you two have a fight?"

"No! Nothing like that." David panicked at her accusation that he might have been involved. "I love Dona. I would never hurt her."

"Sorry, but in cases like this, we look to the people closest to the victim first."

"Victim?"

"If she's been abducted, she's a victim."

David noticed her French accent. "Where are you from?" he asked, hoping to get her on her good side.

"I'm originally from Canada but grew up in North Dakota. Let's start with her full name. Did she live here?"

"Dona Pearson. No, she lives in an apartment downtown."

"Have you checked to see if anyone there has information?"

"Dona was very private. She didn't know her neighbors."

"Could she be trying to avoid you? Maybe she has

a new boyfriend."

The thought shook him up. "No, I don't think so. Besides, Dona's not the type of person who would be out of contact with her family. They haven't heard from her either."

"Sorry. We have to follow every lead."

The officer's demeanor had thawed by the time she took down the information.

"You must be a strong woman to go into this line of work."

"I joined the police academy when I turned nineteen."

"Isn't it dangerous?" he asked, genuinely concerned.

"Nah..." Her voice softened. "I haven't seen any action—mostly mundane things like a kitten trapped in a tree, traffic citations, and domestic disputes."

"What brought you to Florida?"

"I was tired of the snow and the freezing temperatures." Her expression turned serious. "We'll do everything we can to find your fiancée. I'll give you my business card. If you get any new information, or if she gets in touch with you, call me at this number." She scribbled the case number on the card and handed it to him.

"Thank you," he said and walked her to the front door. There was nothing he could do—except wait.

# Chapter 41 | Fighting Back

## The Green Room

---

Joe collected the trays at night when Dona was sleeping. She tried to push the dresser in front of the door, but it was too heavy for her to move. She thought about her father. He'd know what to do. She searched the room, finding nothing except a glass in the bathroom. It was very tiny, but if she set it on its side, it might roll across the floor, and she would hear it. The only safe place was the bathroom, but it didn't lock. She dragged the desk chair inside, thinking she could barricade the door.

With her father fresh in her mind, she dozed off and dreamed of him. His image was so real she could smell his Old Spice cologne and hear him say, "You can't rely on love to save you. You have to do it yourself."

Drenched in sweat, she woke with a start. *I need to stay awake.* Dona felt reached between the mattress and the box spring for the fork she had kept from the food tray. She puffed up the pillows under the blanket. Standing by the side of the door, she stayed still, careful not to move a muscle, waiting for it to crack open and make her escape. As the minutes ticked by, fatigue made her weak in the knees. Tempted to slip back into bed, she resisted and stood firm.

Finally, she heard footsteps in the hall. The door creaked as it slowly opened. Dona took a deep breath and lunged at the figure coming through the door.

"You little bitch," Joe yelled, backing out of the room and slamming the door shut.

It was all wrong. Aiming for Joe's heart, Dona stumbled and stabbed him in the thigh with such force that the fork lodged in his leg.

Dona tried to breathe, but her throat clenched around the lump that settled there. With his blood on her hand, she ran into the bathroom to wash it off, barring the door with the chair.

Joe never entered the room. The hours passed. She wondered what he was planning. Curling up on the floor, she listened for his footsteps, but the house was quiet. She resisted closing her eyes, but soon lost the fight and sank into a restless slumber.

*****

Dona's eyes sprang open in the morning. She peeked into the room. Seeing no one, she looked at the computer screen, waiting for Joe to appear and threaten her.

There was no breakfast tray. There was no lunch and no dinner.

"Where are you?" she yelled, but he didn't reply. *Maybe he left me alone in the house to die, or perhaps I wounded him so severely that he had to go to the emergency room.*

Dona tried to be patient, but time slipped away, and he didn't return. The next day was the same…. And the day after that. Five days passed, but still, no Joe. Alone and starving, she stared at the ceiling, debating whether she should shower. *What's the point?* She didn't care anymore, but she did need to pee.

Feeling dizzy, she thought about crawling to the toilet, but she made it on her own two feet. Weak from hunger, she used her remaining strength to go to the bathroom. She looked at herself in the mirror above the sink. A flicker of memory produced an image of a younger Dona, with healthy brown hair and a natural glow in her skin. Now, she was pale, and her hair hung in greasy strands. Noticing her first gray, she pulled her hair back in a ponytail and splashed cold water on her face.

*Who is this Joe, anyway? What does he want from me?* Dona recalled his questions. Joe, or whatever his real name was, seemed to be focused on getting her to admit something, but what? The conversations she'd had with him were disturbing. She hated the questions that forced her to relive her mistakes and bad decisions. With nothing but time, it was impossible not to reflect on her life.

One of his interrogations was about fatherhood. Angelo came to mind immediately. Could he have been released from prison? Then, there was Richard. After telling him that Steven wasn't his son, he never brought it up again. He had good reason to feel invalidated as a father. She wondered if he thought she'd made it up to hurt him.

Dona never meant to hurt anyone. It just happened that way. She was wishy-washy primarily on relationships, never decisive about anything—except her love for John; he was the man Dona had loved the most. *Someone I dismissed like a piece of trash,* John had said when she told him she was done. He didn't realize it was the hardest thing Dona had ever done. She thought about how her life might have been if she had stayed with him. Maybe she would have been happy running a bed-and-breakfast. She could have put her decorating skills to work. Surely, the walls wouldn't have been green.

Even Dale's customers didn't like green paint. Although Dale was an angry man who thought she belonged back up north with all the other Yankees, she couldn't see him moving past the Mason-Dixon Line. *No—it couldn't be him.*

It had to be someone obsessed with her. Thomas was fixated on her—to the point of being a Peeping Tom. Other women had accused him of stalking, among other nasty things, like stealing their panties and lurking outside their doors. No, not him either. He was still in prison.

David flashed into her mind. When she tried to break up with him, he fell into a black hole of depression, and his moods were unpredictable.

She considered anger a loophole, something she wouldn't tolerate, and a good reason to leave. It would have been easier to break up with David if he were mad at her, but he quickly rebounded and pretended everything was right. His stubborn attachment confounded her. He tried his best to hide his hostility, but it seeped through the cracks.

Dona didn't like the pressure and limited her time with him.

She had forgotten to take her phone off silent once, and he couldn't reach her for hours. He surprised her, showing up at her apartment unexpectedly. He'd let himself in with the extra key to her front door. It freaked her out. *Was he monitoring her?*

# Chapter 42 | Black Impala

## David

---

Three days had passed since the detective took the missing person's report, and David still hadn't heard from the police. They put him on hold whenever he called or sent him to an automated message center. His life was crumbling. It was driving him crazy that he was powerless. He went back to Dona's office building. This time, he wanted answers. The garage was crowded. He drove around, looking for a parking spot. Finally, he saw the red taillights of a vehicle pulling out. He put on his signal and waited, thinking about the cars that he had passed earlier. One of them looked like Dona's Hyundai Genesis.

David parked and walked around the garage again. There was her car. *Maybe she's here at work after all. Perhaps she doesn't want to see me.* His heart pushed its way up into his throat as he started his engine to leave. *How could she do this to me?*

Another driver was waiting for him to back out, but as he shifted into reverse, he slammed on the brakes, went forward, and shut down the engine again. The driver, who thought he was getting a spot, leaned on his horn. David mouthed the words "Sorry" and took a moment to think. If Dona didn't want to see him anymore, she should at least have the decency to tell him to his face. Unsure if he should confront her or not, he reasoned that at least he should know she was okay.

The elevator stopped on the fourth floor. David stepped out and walked past the receptionist.

"Can I help you?" she asked, jumping out from behind the counter and running after him.

"I'm here to see Dona Pearson," he said without looking back.

"Dona's not here. She didn't come in today."

"Did she call in sick?"

"No, but Dona hasn't come into the office in days."

"But her car is in the parking garage." His voice rose. "There must be a mistake."

Dona's boss heard the commotion. "Is there a problem here?"

"Mr. Wilson, this man is looking for Dona."

"As far as I'm concerned, she quit. Dona never called to say she couldn't come to work. She had a full calendar of appointments. I had to give her caseload to another counselor."

"I haven't been able to reach her," David said. "It's been days, but her car is in the parking garage."

"Maybe we should call the police," Mr. Wilson said.

"I already did!"

The entire office buzzed, now focused on Dona's disappearance.

*****

David waited for updates from the police, but they had no leads or the manpower to continue the investigation. He returned to her apartment again, sure they had missed something, but there was still no sign that she had been there. Maybe she ran off to another county. The mail had piled up—utility bills and a letter from Italy. He opened the letter. It was a letter from her cousin.

On his way home, David felt he'd overlooked something. He couldn't shake the notion that he had missed a clue. But what? Then it hit him. The answer wasn't what was in the mail—but what wasn't. Dona disappeared at the end of March. Three weeks had gone by. *Where is her alimony check? She said her ex always sent it on time.*

The phone rang. "Do you have information about my mom?" Steven asked anxiously.

"No, but I have a hunch, and... Have you heard from your father lately?"

"No. What's going on?"

"He hasn't sent the alimony check this month. It's not like him—unless he knows Dona isn't home to receive it."

"Maybe my brother knows something. Richie just returned from Europe."

"I'd like to speak to him. Will you give me his phone number?"

"Sure, but he may not want to talk to you. He's still pissed that she left our dad."

David wrote Richie's number and promised to let

Steven know if he had any new information. Dona had told him her son wasn't happy about the divorce, so they had been estranged for a while. David wasn't sure how he would feel about his mother's new boyfriend calling him, but he had to do it. His stomach rolled into a fist as he pressed the numbers on his phone pad.

"Hi, is this Richie?"

"Yes, how can I help you?"

"My name is David Merritt. I'm a friend of your mother."

"Yes, Steven's told me about you."

"Your mother has gone missing. I'm trying to find her."

"I wouldn't worry. Sometimes she goes off and doesn't tell anyone."

"I don't think that's the case."

"Maybe she doesn't want you to find her?"

"Look, I have some leads. I believe your father may know something about her disappearance."

"What makes you think that?"

"He hasn't sent your mother her alimony check. Your mom told me he's never late."

"You think he has something to do with it?" he demanded. Richie sounded defensive but not surprised.

"Has he ever mentioned your mother in anger?"

"Well, he was devastated when she left him."

"And?" David got the feeling Richie was holding back.

"He's been losing it lately."

"How so?" David hated putting him on the spot.

After all, it was his father, but he sensed Richie knew more than he was saying.

"He's anti-social, bitter about everything. He's stockpiling food." He said he wanted to disappear into the woods and live off the land, the last time I saw him.

"How do you know?"

Richie cleared his throat. "He thinks there's going to be a civil war soon."

"That sounds like a mental issue."

"My father's not crazy!"

"I'm sorry. Please forgive me. That was insensitive, but I'm worried about your mother."

"I'm worried too."

"If you hear from your dad, be sure to ask him where he's living."

"He hasn't called me in weeks, but I'll try to reach him."

"Thanks, Richie." David hung up and drove back to the underground garage to look for clues, but he came up empty.

Richie called him back. "I can't get hold of my father."

"Do you know where he lives?"

"Somewhere in the mountains, that's all I know."

"Yes, but what mountains? The Appalachians— the Rockies?"

"I don't…. Wait. My dad sent me a birthday card last month."

"Do you still have it?" David asked, excited.

"I don't know. I may have thrown it out. I have to look."

David waited while Richie searched.

"Here it is," he said. "I found it. I have the envelope."

"Does it have a return address?"

"Hmm... sort of."

"What do you mean, sort of?"

"It says State Route 17B, Bethel, New York, but there's no house number."

"Is there a Zip Code?"

"No."

"One more question. What kind of car does he drive?"

"I think he has a Chevy Impala. It's black!"

# Chapter 43 | Guns and Knives

## *David*

---

After driving for seventeen hours, David arrived in the Catskill Mountains in Upstate New York. The ink on his pilot's license was barely dry, but he chartered a Cessna 150 from Sullivan County Airport. Inexperienced, he lacked confidence in his flying ability, but it was the only way. His hands shook as he maneuvered the small plane into the sky.

Once airborne, he felt more comfortable and relaxed his chokehold on the yoke. He hadn't had a full night's sleep in two days. Disheveled and looking like he'd used an eggbeater to brush his hair, he tried to remember the last time he shaved. Dona needed him, so he pushed on. He dug into his pocket and found the aspirin pouch. His heart thumped like a drum as he felt the gun. He shoved two aspirin in his mouth and washed them down with warm bottled water.

Flying low over the area known as Bethel, he could see the farms and old buildings dotting the landscape. From the air, some structures seemed about to implode from neglect. Cattle grazed outside of red barns. Large trees gave cover to a few bungalows or residential homes.

Under a hazy sky, he flew low over the treetops, zigzagging north and then south. The only sign of their existence was a dirt driveway leading from the main road. If he calculated wrong, he wouldn't be able to pull up in time. One wrong move and he'd be in serious trouble.

The sun sank lower in the sky. Discouraged, he had to head back to the airport before it was dark. Then he saw it. A black Chevy! He descended lower to get a better look. Yes, it was an Impala; Richie said his father drove the same make. *Could it be?* David's heart beat faster. He felt the blood pumping through his veins. The Impala turned off the road and disappeared. It would be dark soon and harder to find once he was on the ground. He noted the landmarks, judging the location using a massive lake to the south. He pushed the throttle forward, only easing back when the runway was in sight. Using the lever between the seats, David lowered the flaps to shorten his landing roll. After a bumpy touchdown, he jumped out and handed the keys to the waiting agent. "I'm in a hurry," he said.

"I need to check the hours and gauges. It'll only take a moment."

As the minutes ticked by, David grew impatient. Soon, it would be almost impossible to find his markers. The sky was already darkening as a blood-red sun sank behind the mountains.

"I need to go," he begged.

"You're clear," the agent said.

David sprinted to his car at the other end of the

terminal in the dark. He still had to drive another forty minutes to reach the lake. David sped along with the windows open, keeping the fresh air flowing. There were no lights along State Route 17B, which meandered through the hills. A set of headlights bounced over the road every few minutes from an oncoming car. Finally, a sign for White Lake came into view. The house was approximately two miles to the left. Using backroads, some paved, some gravel, he turned off the headlights when he thought he was close, and parked the car on the side of the road. David hesitated before shutting off the engine and getting out of his car. *Maybe I should call for backup.* He reached for his phone, but there was no signal.

The moon hid behind the clouds, giving little light. He could barely see his hands in front of him. It took all his concentration to avoid stumbling or falling into a pothole or ditch. He reached a long driveway with a mailbox, but no name was visible on it. A house was set far back from the main road, overgrown with weeds and bushes. It was the perfect place to hold someone captive. No screams would be heard by anyone passing by. David was getting nervous. *What if Dona is in that house? What if she's dead?*

The clouds lifted, allowing the full moon to light his path. An animal, perhaps a coyote, howled in the distance as he crept closer to the house. The Glock 19 he had taken from his father's display case rested ominously in his pocket. He never liked guns. When he was younger, his father had insisted that he learn how to protect himself. Now, he was ready to use it.

His fists clenched as he approached the old cedar-shingled house. A dim light glittered inside. Keeping low, he crept under the window and peeked in. Nothing was visible, but he heard a television blaring from another room. The next window was higher, and he could barely reach the sill. He hoisted himself up, straining to see past the dining area. A man appeared to be sleeping in a recliner in the living room.

David jumped and walked around the house, staying under the windowsills and out of sight. It was quiet. All he heard was his own breathing. His senses keen, he breathed in the scent of the recently mowed grass and fresh-cut lumber. A strange structure caught his eye — a newly added extension. It lacked windows and had no door. Putting his ear to the outer wall, he heard a woman weeping.

"Dona?"

"David? Is that you?"

"Shhhhh! Be quiet."

"I'm in here, David! Please, please get me out!"

"Hold on. I'm going to find a way inside."

"Please… Don't leave me."

"I'm here. Don't worry. I'll get you out of there."

David ran back to the front window of the house. The man was still asleep. *Maybe I can sneak in through the back door if it's open.* He circled the corner, checking for a guard dog in the yard. David rubbed his jaw and looked around. No dog. He turned the knob slowly, and the back door opened with a slight squeak. The place smelled of marijuana.

He crept through the kitchen and past the living

room, where Dona's abductor was sleeping. As he tiptoed through the hall, a floorboard creaked. David froze. If the man woke up, he'd have to use force. He held his breath and strained to see the man's face. He was still asleep. His long, dark hair looked like it hadn't seen a comb in weeks. His scruffy beard was streaked with white. David gritted his teeth and crept along the dark hall, feeling with his fingers. He came to a door with a large sliding bolt.

"Dona?" he whispered.

"Yes, I'm in here," she cried.

As David slid the lever, metal scraped against metal. The hinges groaned. The door opened, and there she was. He gasped but couldn't exhale. He didn't recognize the woman before him. She was gaunt, and the sparkle in her eyes was gone. Dona fell into his arms.

"I thought I'd never see you again," he whispered.

"Thank God you found me."

He held up his hand for her to be quiet.

"Let's get out of here. Can you walk?"

Dona tried, but her legs buckled.

"I can't!"

David picked her up and hurried out of the room through the narrow hall. This time, he didn't look in the living room.

Soon, they were in the kitchen. Freedom was only a few steps away.

As they neared the back door, Richard lunged in front of them.

"Richard?" Dona screamed. Her captor stood

there, the man who had held her prisoner for almost a month. Horrified, she never imagined the man she had been married to for over twenty years could turn on her this way.

He looked at her with hollow eyes — a haunted stare that shook her to the core.

"You promised you would never hurt me, you bastard!" Pumped with adrenaline, she twisted out of David's arms and charged Richard. Her fists felt like lead as she pounded on his chest.

Richard grabbed an eight-inch hunting knife from the counter. He snaked his arm around and held the knife to her throat. She smelled pot on his hand. Anger again enveloped her as she recalled all the drugs he used while married. Dona bit his hand, feeling the skin part between her teeth. Richard screamed and dropped the knife.

As he bent to retrieve it, David shoved Dona aside and gripped Richard's hand, trying to pry the knife away. Richard pounded the back of David's neck, knocking him to the floor. David continued to grip Richard's hand, holding the knife. Richard punched him in the face, again and again. David twisted Richard's arm, bringing him to his knees. They grappled, slipping and sliding in the blood — whose blood, Dona couldn't tell, but the sight of it made her lightheaded. She noticed a phone on the wall, mere feet away. Lifting the receiver, she dialed 911.

Blood dripping from his hand, David drew his gun and pointed it at Richard. His finger slid down the side of the Glock to the trigger. Richard sprang forward, a crazed look in his eyes.

A shot rang out. Dona crumpled to the floor with the receiver in her hand.

"Hello? Hello? What is your emergency?"

*****

Dona opened her eyes to flashing blue lights. *Where am I?*

Blinded for a moment, she realized she was lying on a gurney in the back of an ambulance.

"David?" she called out. There was no answer.

"Where is David?" she asked the paramedic. "Is he dead?"

"Calm down, lady. Your friend is just fine. He's lucky that knife wound was superficial."

"I heard gunfire. David didn't get shot?"

"No, the bullet lodged in the ceiling, but Mr. Merritt did manage to smack that other guy pretty good with the barrel of his Glock. The guy was still out cold when we arrived. Mr. Merritt is inside getting his hand bandaged."

Dona unbuckled the straps and slid off the gurney.

"You really should get back in the ambulance," the paramedic said. "We need to take you to the hospital."

"I'm not going anywhere." Dona stumbled out of the ambulance and rushed toward the house before the medic could stop her. As she headed toward the front door, she saw Richard and froze.

His head was wrapped in bandages as the sheriff handcuffed him and put him in the back of a cruiser.

Everything made sense now, his refusal to talk with her and the orchestrated losses in her life. Maybe it was all payback, punishment for leaving him. The one thing he hadn't counted on was David.

The paramedic was at her heels when she entered the kitchen. David was sitting at the table. She ran to him and stood behind him like a shield.

"I'll make sure she gets to the hospital," he assured the paramedic.

Another emergency call came over his radio, so he reluctantly agreed.

The ambulance careened out of the driveway, its siren now a whisper in the heavy summer air.

"I'm going to need a statement from the two of you before you leave," the deputy said.

By the time they were free to leave, the sun had risen. Dona squinted and shielded her eyes with her hand against the blinding sunlight.

At last, she was free.

# Chapter 44 | Queen of Hearts

## *David*

---

The sudden rush of oxygen made Dona dizzy. David steadied her and helped her into the car.

"I promised I would get you to the hospital. You need to be checked out."

"I need to go home!"

"No, I'm taking you for treatment. It won't take long. There's a hospital close by here. Then we'll be on the way back to Florida."

Too weak to argue, she agreed.

She opened the window as they traveled along the highway and let the wind whip through her hair.

"I want to call my sons. Can I borrow your phone?"

"Sure. It's in the glove compartment. Steven and Richie will be relieved to know you're safe."

"Wait, their numbers are on my cellphone."

"No worries. Steven's number is on speed dial. I've been in touch with him the whole time. I even spoke with Richie. He helped me find you."

"Really? I'm so glad. Richie and I have been estranged for over a year. I've been sad about that."

"Don't worry. I think he'll come around. He loves you."

After calling Steven, she lay back in her seat and watched the streetlamps whiz by.

"Is everything all right?"

"Yes. Richie is coming to Florida," she said. "He wants me to meet his fiancée."

"I guess I'll finally get to meet him, then." David laughed nervously. "Do you think he'll like me?"

"I'm sure he will."

When the hospital sign appeared, David took the exit. They stopped in front of the emergency room entrance.

"We need a wheelchair," he shouted.

The tech wheeled her to the admission desk to get her name and insurance information, then whisked her through the double doors.

"Can I go with her?"

"Sure, as soon as we get her settled, someone will take you back there."

After twenty minutes, he grew impatient. "Please. My fiancée needs me."

"I'll take you to her."

Dona was hooked to an I.V. when he entered the cubicle. A nurse was feeding her ice chips.

"She's mildly dehydrated, but she'll be fine after she receives intravenous fluids. The doctor will come to see you before you leave to give you discharge instructions."

The doctor prescribed rest and plenty of liquids. It was already dark when they were cleared to leave the hospital. The nurse called for a wheelchair.

"I can walk," Dona insisted.

"Sorry, it's hospital policy. Everyone takes a ride in the chair when they leave."

"I'll get the car," David said as they wheeled her to the front.

He helped her into the car as if she might break.

"I'm fine." She laughed. "Please stop fussing."

"It's my job to fuss over you."

Dona rolled her eyes. "You're such a goofball."

As they pulled away from the hospital, she stared at him. "What's that thing on your face?"

He rubbed his beard. "It's my new look. Don't you like it?"

"It's gross," she teased.

*****

The next day, they arrived at David's house. She could practically taste the ocean's salty air when she stepped out of the car. She hadn't had fresh air in weeks. It made her body feel light and unsteady. David ran around to the passenger side to support her. He unlocked the front door and flipped the switch to turn on the light. A rush of familiar sights and smells enveloped her as soon as she crossed the threshold.

"When was the last time you ate?" he asked.

"I'm not sure."

"Take a nice hot bath while I make you something to eat."

"The bath sounds good, but I don't know if I can

keep anything in my stomach."

"The doctor said you needed to eat."

"I'll try."

He filled the tub and handed her a green towel.

"Don't lock the door," he instructed. "In case you fall or need me for something."

"Yes, Daddy," she kidded.

It was in David's nature to nurture. He'd taken care of his father, and now he needed to take care of her.

Once he was gone, she soaked in the warm tub until her skin pruned.

David knocked on the door. "Are you all right in there?"

"Yes. I'm just drying off."

She slipped into his fluffy white robe on the back of the door and went to the bedroom. Seeing a tray on the side table, she froze, unable to breathe. It was a reminder of her nightmare in the green room.

"It's soup," he said.

His reassuring voice soothed her back to the present. To make him happy, Dona took a few sips of the soup.

"Let's get you tucked into bed." He turned down the comforter and fluffed the pillow.

"You're a good man," she said affectionately.

For a moment, Dona thought having someone take care of her was easier. But only for a moment. She wasn't the same person who went into the green room. Tired of bending herself out of shape for a man, she refused to sacrifice her values on the altar of love.

David played some music and opened the double French doors in his bedroom. As Dona prepared for bed, he came up behind her and caressed her back.

"I've missed you," he said.

She pulled away. "I don't want to make love right now."

"I'm sorry. I know you've been through a lot," he said. "I can sleep in the guestroom if you're more comfortable.

"No." She panicked. "I don't want to be alone tonight."

They slipped into bed. A cool breeze stirred, and the curtains swayed. Dona leaned back against the mound of pillows, and he pulled the covers over them. She rested her head on his chest, afraid to close her eyes, unsure of where she'd be when they opened. The steady thump of his heartbeat soothed her.

*****

Sunshine was streaming through the windows the following morning, blinding Dona as she opened her eyes. As the strength of consciousness took hold, the room came into focus, and she saw David sitting on the edge of the bed. He lingered for a few seconds, staring at her.

"How long have you been watching me?"

"Not long." He brushed his palm along her face. "I made us breakfast and set the table on the balcony."

She stepped outside. The soft morning sun on her face felt good. Waves crashed upon the shore, reclaiming shells and remnants of seaweed that had washed up during the night. She gazed at a sailboat slowly moving across the water.

"It's so peaceful here."

"Have some coffee," he said, pouring it into a cup. "Two creams, no sugar, right?"

Dona laughed.

"It's good to hear you laugh, but what's so funny?"

"Nothing! You're just so sweet, that's all."

"I made French toast. There's also fresh fruit and your favorite yogurt.

"This looks delicious! But I think I'll stick to fruit and yogurt for now." She picked up a strawberry and took a bite. She stirred her coffee even though the cream was already mixed in. She took a sip and then set the glass down on the table.

"I can't believe Richard bought a house in Bethel. He must have followed me there when I saw John and decided it was a good place to escape society." She shuddered. "If it weren't for you, I'd still be locked in that room."

"And I'd still be searching for you, but you're home now!" Leaning forward, he kissed her. "Once you're strong enough, we'll return to your place and get your things."

"Things? I want to go back to my apartment."

"After everything I've been through to find you, I'm not letting you out of my sight. Besides, the doctor said you shouldn't be alone for a while."

I'll stay one more night, but then I must go home."

She had taken a bold step on the path to self-realization.

"By the way, where's my car? Is it still at the office?"

"I used the extra set of keys in your apartment and drove it back to your place when I realized you were missing."

"It had a flat tire."

"I had it fixed."

"You're amazing."

"I would do anything for you."

"My son's arriving today with his fiancée. I told him we'd meet for dinner at their hotel."

"All right, but I don't think we should stay out too late. You need your rest."

"I've been locked up for weeks. I need to get out."

*****

That evening, Dona introduced David to her son. They hit it off, chatting about finances, politics, and their shared love of flying. Steven beamed his approval from across the table. Rebecca's fiancée was delightful, and it was easy to see why he loved her. She could tell he was happy.

"What do you suppose will happen to Dad?" he asked.

"I don't know. One of the officers said they were taking him to the VA hospital."

"I guess they'll treat him there. Maybe he has post-traumatic stress disorder. You know, from when he was in Vietnam."

"That was over twenty-five years ago, although he did begin to act strangely after 9-11. I never connected it."

"Maybe the event triggered some kind of psychotic break," he said. "On the other hand, perhaps he was suffering from substance abuse. He was hooked on pain meds and smoked a lot of pot."

"Well, he wasn't thinking straight, that's for sure," Dona said. "Do you think the divorce had anything to do with it?"

"Don't go blaming yourself now!" Steven said. "It wasn't your fault. He probably would have cracked anyway."

Dona nodded. "Hopefully, he'll get help in prison." She couldn't help feeling sad for Richard. They did have good times during their marriage, and she cared about him despite everything he had done.

"We're leaving tomorrow," Steven said, shaking her back to the present.

"Tomorrow? Why so soon?"

"Rebecca's mother lives in Miami Beach, and we're driving down to surprise her."

"She doesn't know we're engaged yet," Rebecca added, admiring the diamond ring on her finger. "I want to tell her in person."

After dinner, Dona nudged Steven. "Let's take a walk."

They walked out into the lobby.

"It's great to see you, Mom. I've been worried about you."

"For a while, I was worried about me, too. If it

wasn't for David...."

"He seems like a great guy. I'm glad you have someone special in your life."

"Yes, he's special, but...."

"You don't sound too sure."

"I'm not sure he's the right man for me. Don't get me wrong. I love David, and I'm grateful that he saved me. I wish he *were* the right man. I want him to be badly. He's a caring man, but he can be a little overbearing. He has a way of sucking all the oxygen out of a room, and I feel like I'm suffocating."

"Relationships can be tricky."

"I'm still afraid of being alone, but I know I have the strength to get through it. Being locked up in that room forced me to confront my insecurities. It made me realize that my problems stem from me. I guess growing up with an alcoholic father made me codependent."

"Maybe that's why you stayed with Dad for so long."

"When was the last time you spoke with him?"

"I'm not sure, but he didn't sound good."

"How so?" she asked nervously. "Did he say something?"

"Not exactly." Steven grinned. "He's always been a little out there, you know, talking about going off the grid and living in the woods."

"Thank goodness you're not like him," she said.

"Not at all," Steven agreed, giving her a knowing smile.

"Well, I mean—"

"It's all right, Mom. I figured it out years ago."

"Figured what out?"

"Richard isn't my father."

"How—why didn't you say something?"

He shrugged. "It wouldn't have changed anything, but I always felt a distance between us."

"Are you mad at me?"

"I guess I was at one time. That's why I wanted to go out of state to college, but I'm over it now."

"Do you want to know who your real father is?" she asked cautiously.

"No. Not now. Maybe someday."

They walked back inside the restaurant in silence, each lost in their own thoughts. Before they reached the table, Dona reached for his arm to stop him.

"I'm sorry if I hurt you. Can you forgive me?"

Steven smiled. "There's nothing to forgive. You're a good mother, and I love you very much."

His hug reassured her far more than his words.

"As far as David goes... don't live by other people's rules. You're the queen of hearts. Straighten your crown and follow your heart."

*****

Back at David's house, they prepared for bed.

"Don't forget, I'm going home tomorrow."

"I was hoping you'd change your mind."

"You've been so kind to me, but I have to get back to my life, David."

"I understand. You are so special to me. I don't

want to lose you."

A pang of guilt tugged at Dona's heart, but she stood her ground this time.

"You're an important part of my life, but I need time to think things through."

David stroked her hair. "Take all the time you need."

Dona drifted into a lucid dream. "Let me go!" she moaned.

David held her tight, and she thought she heard him whisper, *"I'll Never Let You Go!"*

Some Prisons have no Bars!

Thank you for reading The Green Room by Janet Sierzant. Please take a minute to post a review on Amazon.com.

# Other Books by Janet Sierzant

Gemini Joe
Memoirs of Brooklyn

Sauce on Sunday
An Ancestral to find my Sicilian Roots

A Brooklyn Love Story

Justice Rules

Asunder

A Made Man